High Summons

Eli Celata

Guernsey Memorial Library
3 Court Street
Norwich, NY 13815
www.guernseymemoriallibrary.org

Clean Reads
www.cleanreads.com

HIGH SUMMONS
Copyright © 2016 ELI CELATA
ISBN 978-1-62135-672-1
Cover Art Designed by Cora Graphics

For Giovanni

One

Rochester hadn't always been my home. After growing up in the north end of Boston, New York in any manner was still new. The fit wasn't quite right partly due to the indecisive weather, though Boston wasn't much better. Still, there was something about Rochester which was achingly familiar some days. It had those skyscrapers—the kind I couldn't help but climb with my eyes even if it made my head spin. There were all sorts of corners a kid could get lost in with no clear lines between one ghetto and the next. Less people also made Rochester a bit bigger in feeling even if it wasn't close to a third of Boston's size in space. It was a cozy sweater, and I was going out of my mind in it.

I couldn't just up and leave though. I had worked hard in high school to get into a good college to make my mom proud—and the University of Rochester was awesome, but college made being normal permanent. People attended school, went to college, and got real world jobs. I wasn't people. I had never been people. Telling my mom anything of the sort would have gotten me an earful, but she was mortal. She didn't always get what it was like to have magic and not use it. It was like cutting off an arm. The cityscape didn't help. All these cars and buildings left unattended, but I couldn't just crumple them up or walk up them supernatural style without weird looks and the nightly news suspecting Russians. They made it look so simple in the comics.

Honestly, there wasn't a day I didn't think about those mythical traveling circuses from the 1940s where I could run away and just manipulate fire or levitate for the rest of my days. My mom was the only thing keeping me normal, and she'd lost a lot to do so. Being a single parent to a mix-raced child out of wedlock was tough enough, but a wizard's son? Yeah, I wouldn't wish me on anyone, especially five-year-old me making an army of marching melted chocolate soldiers. We never got the stain out.

Sitting in front of my computer in the café, I twitched glancing between the clock and my roommate who was engrossed in the business management assignment. There had to be something better to do than reading articles on how not to screw up employee morale. I flipped my pencil up into the air and caught it on my nose. I even let it float above my face a few centimeters just to see if I would get caught, but somehow, nobody was looking. Nobody was ever looking when I used magic. Well, my mom saw me do it, but it just wasn't the same. She'd seen my dad do magic. I wasn't impressive in comparison except for the chocolate soldiers.

I set the pencil on the table and rolled it back and forth over the pages I should have been reading when my roommate, Tyson, glanced up at me with his familiar brown glare. "If you're bored, go back to the dorms."

"You drove," I retorted, and he rubbed the bridge of his nose. I don't even think his nose was big enough for it to do much besides remind me I was trying his patience.

"It's not too far. Seriously, Jon, some of us actually have to study," Tyson said. I couldn't fault him for his frustration. He was working against the odds just as much as I was, socioeconomic and all, without magic to make it feel mundane.

"One B isn't going to kill your grade for the course," I pointed out, but I shoved my stuff into my backpack and stood before he could retort. "I'm going out of my mind here. I'll see you back at home."

Tyson sighed. "Fine, whatever, man. I can't afford to lose my scholarship."

"You got in with football."

"Hey now." He waved me toward the door of the café. "Get your passably white self out of here."

The door shut slowly behind me as I headed onto the streets hoping maybe I'd get a chance to spin some air or something before locking my magic back down. Wandering down the street looking for a sign to point me to where I was, I found myself in a rather odd part of the city. Rochester was filled with small businesses; however, they were not small building-wise. They were ordinarily parts of much larger areas such as the bottom floor of a huge building. This street was not normal. There was a row of houses pressed close together with small, barely one-person-wide alleys between them. It wasn't the whole street—just a short bit toward the end.

One of the houses which had been turned into a store was a sort of an uncanny, ugly pink-purple color. I couldn't help but cringe at the sight even in the dark. A black lantern hung down from a curved bar of metal above the door lending some light to the old fashion wood sign swinging out from near the door which had "Ardireallius Magieus" written across the black wood in fancy silver letters. The store was situated in the exact middle of two street lamps, so it had the least light shining on it of all. Even with the dim light, the crisp neon paint shown vividly like a beacon. Three stone steps, the bottom of which was cracked, led up to a doormat which said, "welcome upon invitation only," and a dull blue door with no knob but three locks and an old fashioned ram's skull knocker. The knocker seemed almost alive. It was a dull off-white shade, and the horns were a swirling mixture of browns. The ring was clenched in the knocker's skull-like jaw. It was copper, as were the locks.

Again, I had never been into architecture, but the shape didn't so much catch my eye. The oddness hanging all about the place did. There was an iron rail on one side of the stone steps and the remnants of another on the opposite side. A large bay window stood to the left of the doorway. The glass seemed thick, and as I leaned to get a closer look, there was an odd shimmering effect. I shifted my weight to my right foot and then to my left. As I did, a giant infinity symbol shimmered across each pane of glass. I shifted my weight back to my right and the symbols vanished. I repeated this little trick a few times before my brain

caught up with me, and I shook my head walking onwards away
from the store. Passing the alley on the opposite side of the store,
I stopped dead in my tracks.

Normal was not my thing. Normal was for people who
didn't see things at night or in shadows out of the corners of
their eyes. From day one, I had seen monsters, and if my mother
hadn't seemed just as scared of them, I might have believed I was
insane, but she knew they were real. The monsters were as real as
the strange abilities I had. If I was scared, I would find myself
home within a minute even if I was miles away. When I got angry
at somebody, something bad would happen to them. At first, I
thought it was all coincidence, and even at the age of eighteen, I
was certain some days I was insane and couldn't make the water
float around the bathroom or the fire become the shape of a
dragon. Then I walked past the shop and saw another monster,
but this time, I wasn't the only one looking at it.

It wasn't ugly; in fact, it was almost pretty. Long knotted
black hair pooled about its narrow shoulders. Pale skin pulled
tight about its cheekbones. It swirled, unable to move on its own,
completely at the mercy of the whims of the tiniest breeze. It
wore black robes: tattered and worn as if decaying. The fingers of
the hands of the creature were long and skeletal, as were the
arms. Its lips were chapped; its eyelashes covered in ash. It smiled
at me almost gently. Tears filled its eyes, and magma flowed
down. The flesh crackled, burning away only to reform. It
reached for me, and I stopped in my tracks. Its mouth opened,
and a swirling vortex sat where an esophagus should have been.
Stars and planets swirled in orbit around a black hole slowly
swallowed them, one by one. There the beauty ended, and the
fear began. Except the monster wasn't like the usual ones who
floated around without acknowledging me or anyone else. This
monster was fighting someone.

The man was decent height though a bit shorter than most,
maybe around five eight or nine. He wore skinny, dark-wash
jeans with a white, button-up shirt with the sleeves rolled up to
his elbows. He was using a flame thrower on the monster except
the flame thrower was his hand. Meaning, the fire was coming

out of his skin like it was nothing. I've manipulated fire, but to create fire so intense was incredible. His bright white hair was highlighted by the light as was the tanned tone of his skin. He couldn't have been more than twenty-five, but he was the most awe-inspiring guy I'd ever seen. This was made even more so considering, when the fire stopped, there was no more monster. It melted away, and he just stretched like it was his warm up.

Spinning around, he swaggered over to a nearby motorcycle covered in glow-in-the-dark tribal designs. He hopped on, riding off in the opposite direction all within a couple of seconds. If it hadn't been for the light catching my eye, I might have missed seeing the only person who could possibly understand. I knew I wasn't alone. My dad was a wizard, but I'd never gotten a chance to talk to him about it. He was gone before I was two, taking his knowledge and whatever others existed with him. After sixteen years alone, this was it. There was not even a doubt in my mind. Tomorrow, I had to come back.

Two

The street was almost the same in the late afternoon as it had been the night before. There weren't too many people near the shop though the rest of the sidewalk on the same side had plenty. A few crossed the road to walk around me as I stood outside the store which didn't have a ram's head anymore. From the cracked stone step to the neon pink hue of the paint, everything else was the same except the ram. Where the skull had been, a small pewter doorknob sat with an innocent dullness like it was saying, "Yeah, I was totally here the whole time."

Jumping up the steps, I opened the door and a low bell rang throughout the store. The inside of the book store was so boring compared to the door and window I almost yawned. Shelves lined the walls. Shelves created halls in the larger area, and to the right upon entry was a counter with a register and bags which said, "Thank you for shopping!" with an odd smiling face beneath the black lettering. A picture hung over the counter of an old man with a large smile and eyes so blue they almost looked white.

The books ranged from non-fiction to children's, and Danielle Steel had a shelf all to herself along with Stephen King and, oddly enough, some guy named W. K. Strider. His books looked well-worn compared to the rest, and I wondered if the owner of the store was trying to sell his own books since I had never heard of Strider. All of those books were just what I saw from the foyer of the place. The floors were dark wood, and the ringer above the door was shaped like an angel. Not the sort of angel usually caught hanging out in stores either. This angel was a warrior with armor over his dress and a sword. Numerous doorstoppers were lined up like tiny soldiers behind the door and faded chalk lines were on the back of the door.

On the opposite side of the bay window were a single table and two wooden chairs facing outwards. Maybe it was the daylight, and maybe things just looked different on the inside, but no matter how I leaned, the eights didn't show up. Turning back to the shelves, I wandered through the mazelike setup without any sign of the guy from last night. I circled back around to the front of the shop and nearly ran into this dude carrying a huge box of notebooks and other stationary materials.

"Sorry!" I said holding up my hands and backing away when I noticed the white eyebrow raised at me from behind metal rectangular glasses was, in fact, the same guy from last night.

"No problem," he retorted and moved on behind the counter.

While he unpacked the box and set up the remainder of the display on the small shelves besides the register, I stared in shock. He hadn't been wearing anything intimidating before, and he certainly wasn't now. The jeans seemed about the same, but instead of a dress shirt, he had a navy sweater with professor patches in light brown on the elbows. He was seriously the least threatening sort of person I had ever seen though he did have a pretty wicked eyebrow ring on the right with runes carved into what looked to be bone. Plus, there was what looked to be a tattoo on the left side of his neck. All in all, I thought I had been rather successful in tracking down my mystery monster hunter even though I had just gone to the same place and gotten extremely lucky.

He seemed to know I was staring and leaned with his elbows on the counter. He didn't say anything because maybe it wouldn't be cool or something, but he just watched me right back as if to say I should just spit it out already. I wasn't entirely sure what to say. Honestly, I kept envisioning the conversation in my head turning absolutely belly up with another person thinking I was mental with some sort of deranged version of monster schizophrenia—well, just schizophrenia then. Eventually, I swaggered over to the counter, and he smirked.

"Do you have the latest Butcher novel?" I wanted to smash my face into the nearest surface. Seriously, I was a coward.

He pointed over to the shelf I had been standing by only moments ago. "Right back there."

"Great." I tried to recover. "Thanks."

I trudged over and picked up the book I already had a copy of and debated whether I had to go through with buying the thing when he called out in rough voice, "Not a monster."

I turned around. Surely, he couldn't have been talking to me. No, he was staring straight at me with this dull sort of know-it-all look and one raised eyebrow and a cocky smirk. I put the book on the shelf and walked back over to him. He leaned away from the counter with his hands holding onto the edges sizing me up. At six-foot two, I was rather impressive despite my lanky appearance otherwise. I knew exactly what he was seeing. A face with hazel eyes, shaggy, dark blond hair, and a kind of latte skin-tone finished off with an awkward nose which wasn't flat or pointed but somewhere in between and just a little too big. The stubble around my jaw ensured he couldn't think me prepubes-cent. I hoped my hole-covered jeans, black converse, and U of R sweater didn't make him think I was just some dumb frat boy.

"What do you mean?" I asked trying to seem as nonchalant as he was before his eyebrow lowered, and I added, "What was it then?"

"Demon."

"Demon?" I repeated doubtfully.

"Demon." He nodded. "Amswae—though most humans call it a banshee."

"So, demons." He gave me the look suggesting he was get-ting sick of repeating himself, so I quickly continued. "How can you see them? I mean, I see them—but no one ever—and the fire thing." I pointed to my hand like it actually needed some sort of explanation.

"How have you survived this long?" he asked looking at me

with a slight grimace. "Magic. It's all magic. You're what, eighteen? You have a teacher, right? Master?"

"Um, plenty of professors," I offered, and he look mildly put out with pursed lips and narrowed eyes before he reached a hand out.

"Jordan," he said. It took me a moment, but I shook his hand when I realized he was saying his name as an introduction.

"Jonathan—uh, most people actually call me Jon," I informed him.

A light sparked in Jordan's eyes then vanished just as quickly. Jordan smirked again nodding as our hands fell apart from each other. "You have magic. Otherwise, you wouldn't have seen the fire or the demon."

"So there's a mist!"

Sighing, he glared. "This is going to get complicated if you keep interrupting me. You have magic, kid." I frowned at the word. I wasn't a kid, and he certainly wasn't too much older than me. "You need a teacher, or you'll eventually get yourself killed."

"Probably not, the demons don't notice me normally," I replied, and he seemed a bit startled.

He stared at me as if thinking for a moment before he gestured to the cord around my neck, "Family amulet—your father's?"

My eyes widened in shock, and he smirked. Pulling out the iron coin hung from the leather string, I was stupefied. "How did you know?"

"The amulet has protected you because you haven't been learning magic. As long as you remain ignorant of summoning, you can just wear it for the rest of your life with only high-powered demons being a risk. You're older than most during their First Summoning. In the United States, your chances of getting killed are rather small—lights and development and all urbanization's great wonders—but you have a good chance of avoiding the Hell spawn who'd still notice you," he explained, and though he observed the coin without blinking for the entirety of the explanation, he never reached out to touch the metal.

"But I could learn magic." Maybe I had a bit of a habit of ignoring details meant to keep me safe.

"Yeah, I could teach you if you wanted. Not your master though—I don't have time." Jordan leaned against the counter. "I'm only in town for a job. Afterwards, I'm hitting the road again. If you aren't serious enough about this to come along, it would be better if you just keep being ignorant."

I had so many questions I didn't know where to even start. "It had to be through my dad, didn't it? He had to have magic because my mom doesn't have it. She knew about it, but it had to have been him, right?"

"Your name is Jonathan Blythe, right?" he retorted, and my jaw dropped.

"How did you..."

He nodded. "I knew your father. Grew up with him back in Iceland."

"How do I know you're telling the truth?" This was too lucky. I had been looking for clues on my dad in my spare time since I was eight and realized there was a chance he was still alive somewhere.

"Your mother will know who I am. Call your mother," he said. "Call her. Tell her you met Jordan Ostairius. She'll confirm it." I pulled out my cell phone to call, but he held up a hand. "Go home. Think about your options. Talk to you mother, and then you come back here tonight at nine if you want to become my apprentice. Otherwise, only come here to pick up books."

Jordan went back to setting up the notebooks, and I walked out of the store in a daze. I had thought I was lucky when Jordan was a stranger with magic who saw the demons. To find out he also knew my dad was insane. He was way too young to have actually grown up with my dad, but if there were only a few magical people in the world, I wouldn't be shocked if they knew each other anyways. On the way back to my dormitory, I dialed my mother's work number uncertain if her shift was done. When her desk rang back with a pre-recorded voice mail message, I quickly called her cell phone. It rang twice before she picked up.

"Hey sweetie, what's—" I didn't have the patience to wait for her to finish saying hello.

"I met Jordan! You know Jordan Ostairius! The Jordan-with-Dad Jordan!" I knew I was talking way too fast, but the excitement was overwhelming. I paused and waited for her to respond. My entire skin felt like it was buzzing in anticipation.

"Oh."

She had never sounded so small. My mom was superwoman. She could sew any Halloween costume a kid could dream up and had never made me feel like having no dad was a disadvantage. Even when my grandparents had tried to get back involved in our lives when I was six, she didn't blink beneath their constant, thinly veiled insults and didn't hesitate to cut them off again when they turned a bit too much of their burn-for-eternity mentality at me for being born out of wedlock even though I had been baptized at some point.

"Mom?"

"It's fine," she told me though she didn't sound fine at all. "Okay, it's good even. I should have contacted him back when you first told me about the monsters when you were twelve. I—" There was the sound of a deep, shuttering breath over the phone. "It's good."

"So, he's legit?" I asked turning the corner to walk down the street to campus.

She sighed. "What did he say to you?"

I waited for the light to turn to cross the street as I said, "He grew up with Dad in Iceland. He talked about magic and offered to train me."

"Oh!" This time, she sounded pleased like whatever the first exclamation had feared hadn't been what had happened. It made me wonder exactly what she had thought he would say as I dashed through the intersection. "Yes, it's all true. Training though? Are you sure?"

"I think so, yeah. I mean, wouldn't it be better if I could control what I can do? Plus, maybe he knows where Dad is," I replied making my way across the campus grounds to my dormitory.

"Jon—your father…" She paused as if trying to figure out how to have this conversation again. "I don't want you getting mixed up in demon hunting just because your dad did it. It's dangerous."

I stopped in my tracks processing what she had said. "What? Demon hunting? I didn't say anything about the monsters being demons."

I could feel her silently swearing over the phone. "There are a lot of things about your father I haven't exactly told you for your own safety. He wasn't the greatest person, Jon, despite what you might want to think. He was powerful and dangerous and entirely devoted to his job which is why he left. Yes, he thought he was protecting us, but he had to have known you would have magic. He always told me those with magic had to either abandon their powers or hunt demons; otherwise, they become the hunted."

"So what you're saying is you didn't tell me about Dad because of what? Of the chance I might want to learn magic, and learning means I'd have to hunt? Jordan turned his hand into a flame thrower! If he teaches me, I think I'll be safe. Plus, he never mentioned hunting!" I informed her trying to keep my voice low to avoid any questionable glances from the students I was walking by and to avoid her turning this back around on me for yelling at her.

"Don't say yes until you know for sure you don't have to hunt. Hunting means no stable job which means nothing you wanted from a place of your own to consistent food on the table. No one pays for demons to be killed anymore, especially in the United States. I did what I did to protect you, and your father agreed it was necessary," she said, and I could hear her engine stop and her cell phone disconnect from her car's stereo system. "Jordan is—" She seemed uncertain how to end the phrase but settled on— "Powerful. There are levels of magic users. I don't know the exacts, but magic waters down with non-magic, and Jordan was a pure blood."

"Meaning?"

"There will be a lot he can do you won't be able to. You need to get a better explanation from someone who knows before saying yes. Magic users take deals tremendously seriously, and an apprenticeship is a deal," she told me. I scanned my ID card and opened the door to my dorm.

"I know. I've got a meeting with him tonight," I told her though I left out it was rather late in the day in the city rather than on campus.

"I don't think this is a good idea, but you deserve to make this choice on your own." She sounded utterly defeated.

Standing in the lobby, I felt the weight of her tone fall squarely on my shoulders. "I'm not going to be like him, Mom."

"Being like him isn't what worries me," she whispered. "I love you. You be careful."

"I will, Mom. I love you too." The click of the call ending echoed in my mind having swept away my enthusiasm. Pushing the button for the elevator, I considered, rather briefly, not going, but there were too many questions to ignore the invitation. I had to go even if I ultimately said no.

Three

The shop was unavoidably eye catching at night, and Jordan held the door open for me. Where the doorknob had been, the ram's skull sat instead. Noticing it caught my eye, Jordan turned it with a wink.

"Just an illusion," he explained. The eye sockets glowed, shifting as if watching us. "The owner of the shop thinks it wards off evil."

"Owner?" I asked as he shut and locked the door behind me.

"On vacation."

Gesturing at the picture of the old man, he grabbed a piece of chalk from the top of the doorframe. The back of the door was covered in quickly erased smudges which he neatly drew over. When he was done, a sideways figure eight remained.

"What's with the symbol?" I pointed to it as he put the chalk back where he had found it.

"Draw a lemniscate on the door and the demons can't get in. It's a ward," he said walking over to sit in one of the wooden chairs by the window.

"This isn't me saying yes," I told him as I sat in the chair beside him. "This is me checking out my options."

"You're here, meaning your mother confirmed what I said. Whatever concerns she expressed didn't deter you, so I doubt tonight will stop you," Jordan said. His eyes never left the window.

With all the shop's lights off and no sun, the strange shimmer returned to the window. Curving figures vanished and appeared with each step. Lemniscates interlocked throughout the panes. In the strange twisting of light, runes surrounded the shadows along the window sill right before the glass and up around the edges.

"If I learn magic from you—if I become your apprentice, will I have to hunt demons?"

He glanced over at me before looking back out the window as if waiting for something. "Yes."

"Oh, um, hunting doesn't seem ...*safe*." I deserved the disgusted sneer twisting his face at my lame response, but I also deserved an answer. "I mean, why?"

"Back in the first days of man, there was a witch." Jordan spoke like he was reading from a child's storybook. "She had three sons, but when her husband died, she could not protect them. She sold her soul—the souls of her sons and their children and their children's children up until the end of time—for power enough to keep her sons safe."

"Her what?" My mind melted like a bolt of lightning had struck.

Jordan nodded. "Her soul. She made a deal with the Devil. Most of those living with magic today can trace a line from their blood to hers." He waved his hand. "Her eldest son died in a river. She could not save him, but she drained the river dry. Her second son died of starvation when the crops failed to grow, and she could not summon them without the water. As her youngest son lay emaciated in her arms, she realized she'd been blind. A man came from Heaven and offered her a promise of redemption if she would protect humanity from the powers of Hell. She accepted. The water flowed. The crops grew, and it was good."

"'A man came from heaven?' Big H Heaven?" Doubt colored my tone.

Jordan didn't answer. Instead, he stood wandering to the stationary display and picked out a black faux leather notebook. Tossing the book at my face, he laughed when I fumbled it, barely managing a catch. I held it aloft in celebration of my success. The pen he'd sent trailing after hit me square in the nose.

"The first night of an apprenticeship is called The Viewing." He paused and tapped the cover of the notebook. I scrambled to open to the first page. Uncapping the pen, I wrote down what he had said.

"Sorry."

Sitting back down, he shifted to stare out the window. "All those with magic are given a choice: hunt demons, give up their magic, or be hunted and damned to Hell."

"So if I don't hunt, I'll get sent to Hell?"

Jordan shook his head. "There's always giving up your magic. No more manipulating elements. No more dumb luck."

Giving up my magic wasn't an option. The electricity beneath my skin was me. Sure, it wasn't vital. I could live a generally full life without it, but it wasn't the same. Magic was like a second appendix. I knew the little jerk could turn against me, but I liked keeping my organs internal. When I had been lonely and feeling like scum visiting the grandparents, I had magic. My paper airplanes flew around the room whenever I wanted. For those few moments, I could pretend my dad was there. Magic was my dad. I couldn't cut it out any more than I could give up on the idea of him coming home.

"There's a classification system for magic users, right?" I asked avoiding Jordan's piercing gaze.

Jordan nodded. "Psychics, magicians, warlocks, mages, and wizards in order respective to power. Psychics can use runes and sometimes have visions of current events. Magicians do elemental manipulations but cannot league walk and have more limited endurance than warlocks. Mages have a greater endurance than warlocks. Mages speak in tongues. Wizards can do the aforementioned as well as warping and a bit more depending on the wizard." His eyes narrowed as he glanced at me. "There are two orders: the Daughters of Tinashe and the Sons of Snorri. The Daughters are a matriarchy with hunting trios. They deal more in higher level demons and are the most functional governmental body for magic users. The Sons are smaller and deal in relics and odd cases."

He gestured toward the window as a swirling cloud passed by the glass. The faceless cyclone spun away and proceeded to incinerate itself beneath one of the street lights. Glancing at Jordan, I doubted it was anything more than just a tiny trick of the wind.

Jordan said, "Enenra—not a threat, but a demon nonetheless. It's more likely to get itself killed like you saw than to kill you."

"How many demons are there?" There couldn't be too many, or so I thought. Jordan tilted his chair back and grabbed a book from a nearby shelf which he handed to me. "*The Demon Bestiary?* Seriously?"

"It's useful, and it'll save you a bit of writing."

I flipped through the book. It was as thick as a dictionary and filled with entry after entry on demons like an encyclopedia. There was no author's name on the front or in the back inside cover, and the rest was formal looking with a rough exterior material and the title inlaid in a gray metallic tone. The pictures were all drawings or sketches with sections broken down into threat level out of ten, most common habitats, some history, and how to deal with them. I had a feeling this book would get more use than any of the text books I had bought at the beginning of the semester.

"How are demons made?" I wondered aloud.

Jordan chuckled. Maybe he just wasn't used to talking so much, but his voice was disturbingly rough. "When humans go bad, we turn into voids. When angels fall, they turn into demons, but just like humans can parcel out their souls to different demons, some demons are only pieces of angels shattered from the pain of the fall."

"Can the angels, the shattered ones, can they reform?" I didn't and still don't know why I started with it, but the question felt oddly vital.

"In theory."

"Where do demons come from?" He gave me a strained sideways glance. "The Hell where the people go and the demon Hell—do they exist? Are they the same?"

"Same. Though demons can go to Hell, the location, they're always in Hell internally," he replied.

I continued after taking a moment to scribble down Jordan's answers thus far in the notebook. "So—are humans defenseless against demons? I mean, they can prey on normal people, right?"

"No one is defenseless," Jordan assured me. "The light of a soul can be used to destroy a demon. You would not believe how many demons have met their ends at the hands of a tiny, terrified child who believed without a doubt that mummy or daddy would come in and save the day."

I wrote everything down in furious chicken scratch. "Why do demons want souls?"

"Demons don't want souls, and they can't possess humans without magic as those souls already have an owner if they go dark. A soul can be bright, but just like a star, it can collapse in upon itself to become a void," Jordan said.

"Like a black hole!" I exclaimed.

"Abstractly, yes. They add the void to their own, and it allows them to cross over for longer lengths of time and gains them power in Hell," Jordan explained. He drummed his fingers against the table before adding, "With enough effort, a soul can be redeemed." Jordan shifted in his chair to face the window. "It's about time; pay attention."

I wanted to keep asking questions, and it irked the crap out of me I couldn't. Putting my feet up on the window sill, I forced my legs not to twitch as I sank into the chair. My eyes glazed over with the effort of staying still. Jordan was sitting back and looking all too cool for the world. I was nearly crawling out of my skin in excitement to see what would happen next. Because of it, I almost missed the next demon to pass.

The wind picked up a little. Just enough to sort of whirl around. An old man in a trench coat walked past the window on the opposite side of the street. He was lanky and hunched over, so it was hard to judge height. Nothing about the man seemed off. He then looked up toward the window. His face shimmered and twisted. The contortion matched the patterns in the glass. His face peeled like a bad sunburn. Where a nose should have been, the demon had a hole instead. His eyes twinkled—all four of them. By the time he smiled with his two mouths, there was no doubt he was a demon.

"Dorota always look generally the same. Old man form, covered up in lots of clothing. They have twice as many eyes as they
have mouths and three times as many arms," Jordan narrated as
the demon passed.

"How do you deal with Dorota?" I asked trying to catch up
writing.

Jordan shook his head. I knew it was probably in the bestiary, but I wanted his take on it anyways. He had made his hand a
flamethrower against an Amswae. Surely, he had some ideas
about fighting demons which weren't exactly conventional. Then
again, maybe turning a hand into a flame throwing machine was
what all demon hunters did.

"The shadow is the void, or the void is in the bottommost
mouth." He rummaged for a moment in his jacket and pulled
out a solar powered flashlight. Jordan held it toward me and
continued when I took it. "The light would be enough to kill it
either way. But if the void is in the mouth, you have to get it to
open it first, and it won't open it unless it doesn't know you have
the torch."

I was going to ask what I should have with me at all times.
What the basic arsenal of a magic user was, but then another
figure passed by the glass. Once I was concentrating again, I
noticed it wasn't just one figure. There was a dark cloud of small
creatures. I leaned forward to get a better view. They looked like
black beetles with tiny red eyes. If it wasn't for the formation of
them, I would have ignored their existence. They swarmed in the
form of a small child.

"Those are Baoht. Rarely travel alone. Void beneath their
wings. Small void so the line has to be aimed perfectly for it to
hit the void while the wings are moving." Jordan smirked and
flipped a small laser pointer through his fingers. As the cloud
moved forward, he hit the button and a line of red light went
through the window. It hit the reflective surface of a nearby street
sign and one of the tiny Baoht screeched and was gone. There
was no dust. There was no blood. It simply ceased to exist. He
held the laser pointer out to me.

I wasn't exactly in a state of shock, but I was still a bit surprised when none of the other Baoht seemed to notice what had happened. I took the laser pointer and stuck it in my pocket. "Why aren't they stopping? Don't they know one of them got hit?"

Jordan glanced at me as if measuring his words against me before speaking. "Given a choice, most demons will use each other as shields against an attack. Only the most powerful are capable of such emotions toward other figures, and even then, most of them don't practice."

I watched the swarm flutter around the lights, and a few more died as they were pushed out of the way by others. "So, does it mean those who care are more likely or less likely to be a problem?"

"I can think of at least one demon who would definitely be more likely. There are three demons who were born: Mammon, Orpheus, and Berith." Jordan paused and watched a figure cross the street. "Just human," he told me after a moment.

"I thought Orpheus was a Greek poet." I glanced between the window and Jordan. The human passed without trouble, leaving our sightline empty of anything save the other side of the street.

"Orpheus is a name. Thousands of men named Orpheus. Probably won't see him topside. Definitely won't be going downstairs to sneak a peek." He shivered. "Demon Orpheus hasn't left Hell since the Romans. Lilith—his mom—is protective. He's weak. She had him with Beelzebub. She probably would kill him for Mammon—son by the Devil. Favoritism," he said studying the street. "Mammon doesn't give two cents though—about her or anything else."

"Wow, nice guy," I scoffed.

Jordan shrugged making a noncommittal huff before continuing. "Orpheus is a mama's boy. Loves her. Hates his dad. Hates everyone else. He's more passionate than his brother."

"What about Berith? Lilith's third kid?"

"Berith... well..." Jordan fidgeted in his seat. "He's been known to kill other demons to avoid returning to Hell." I reread my notes and glanced through the window at an approaching form. Jordan pointed toward the figure. "Pay attention."

"Why are so many different types of demons passing?"

Jordan laughed, and his laughter rattled the glass as the book cases glowed as if trying to hold the books prisoner on their shelves. He was more than I could ever be, and I was far too entranced to be envious of so much power. He was swiftly becoming my idol, and I knew I was wandering into dangerous territory. I didn't know him. Jordan seemed about as survivalist as a demon on some levels. I was there likely more because of my father than because of his interest in passing on knowledge to the next generation. He was a wolf in sheep's skin, and the fact I had to keep reminding myself of his untrustworthiness made me nervous. Jordan never answered, simply laughing and gesturing toward the oncoming demon.

It was the ugliest little thing I had ever seen. Its skin looked like burnt tapioca speared over the wire frame of an anorexic teddy bear. The ears were pointed instead of rounded, and it had large humanoid eyes. They were a golden color in the iris. It was three feet of slime with claws and wings like a vulture. The feathers were molting off its back and sticking to its skin. Glancing around nervously, the demon stopped its movements in the middle of the road right in front of the window. I raised a hand to see if it could see me, and it gave me a look like I was the most nauseating thing it had ever seen. Jordan grabbed my hand and slammed it down against the arm of the chair I was sitting in.

"What is that thing?" My voice cracked, and I could feel an odd sense of panic rising. I had been fine a moment ago. "What is it doing? Is it—"

"The thing is a Craterr. They are often called the scouts of Hell." He removed his hand from my wrist. "It will move along shortly. Stay calm; it can't get through."

I took a deep breath and looked at the Craterr once more. An aura seemed to leak from it like steam. An odd feeling crept over me. Focusing my eyes for the first time – not in a physical manner, I was already focusing them. I mean in a magical manner. All of a sudden, I saw it wasn't exactly the anorexic, tapioca-covered teddy bear I had thought it was. A humanoid demon stood in its place. The giant vulture wings were still there, and he wore the armor like the Roman legionnaires in the old movies my mom liked to watch. Black leggings and tunic were covered by the metal cuirass. Small wisps of black hair stuck out from beneath its helm which had a black crest. A lock of it was grown long and hung braided between its wings. Tribal markings encircled its left upper arm and a ribbon of white cloth was wrapped around its head, covering its eyes. From beneath the helm came two pairs of pointed ears. They twitched, turning in different directions. I knew then freaking out might be a good idea, despite Jordan's calm disposition.

"Are you sure the demon is a Craterr?" I asked slowly as I sketched the demon hidden behind another demon's guise.

I swear I saw a glint of pride in Jordan's eyes at the question. "No, I'm quite certain it's an Evoca taking the form of a Craterr in order to hunt. While the Devil and upper level demons often use Craterr to scout, Evoca work exclusively for the Devil. Craterr don't have wings, but Evoca rarely are able to hide their wings due to their need to see with them. Only extremely powerful Evoca will risk the loss of their sight for extended periods of time. Generally, they stay in legions like Baoht. When they're alone, they're looking for a quick kill."

Jordan stood and walked toward the window. The creature's ears focused in on the shop, and one of the wings opened and turned slightly so the inside was angled toward us. The feathers looked as though they each had an eye-like pattern. When the feathers bristled, the eyes moved though the feathers kept still after the single shiver. Every single one stared right at us.

"What do we do? Can it get through the glass?" I leaned back in my chair as Jordan stuffed his hands in his pockets and stared at the Evoca.

"Stay here."

"What? Where are you going?" I nearly yelled as he walked toward the door. I jumped to my feet and took a step to follow him, but a glower told me to stay put. "But it can come in if you open the door, right?" I called after him as he opened the door and closed it quickly behind him.

Turning back to the window, I fumbled to feel out where my chair was. I sat with my elbows on my knees staring at the ground almost too panicked to glance up. A few deep breathes later, I dared a peek. The demon's attention was completely on Jordan as he waltzed up to it. He said something. I saw his lips moving but had no idea what was happening. The demon turned both its wings toward Jordan and licked its lips. Its tongue was a bright blue against its ash colored mouth. Jordan made a vague gesture toward the store, and a wing moved, so the eyes were looking toward me. The Evoca nodded, and its feathers bristled before its wings widened as it turned back to Jordan as if trying to intimidate him. The Craterr guise fell away.

Right then was the first time I saw a void. Even though the others had voids too, they'd been too small or hidden. With a twitch of its wings, the Evoca was air-born. Instead of a shadow which should have shrunk as it rose, an empty hole remained. Darkness swirled inside. Pulsing with a life of its own, the void glimmered like ink.

Jordan shook his head holding out his hand. I couldn't see what was there, but I could see it glowing. Not overly bright, but a decent light. He gently tossed the source of the light toward the void. The next thing I heard was a shriek. It rattled the glass and shook the books on their shelves, and as swiftly as it came, it ended. Everything stilled. Unlike the Baoht, the Evoca remained alive. Shaking and trembling, but alive nonetheless. Feathers were missing from its wings, and it seemed to flutter between being visible and fading from view. I suppose it was shimmering between Earth and Hell. I wrote a note down to ask Jordan, and when I glanced back up again, the Evoca was gone. I didn't hear the door as Jordan slipped into his seat.

Before I could even open my mouth to form the question, Jordan's eyes flicked down to my notebook. "Yes."

"What was the thing that you—" He held up a tiny little ball. It was the kind out of a quarter machine. "...seriously?"

Jordan squeezed the ball, and it glowed. Dropping it on the ground, he let it bounce and then caught it. "The simplest things can bring the best results. One ball and good aim can last you awhile." He put it back in his pocket. "You'll get one when you can aim, if you stay."

I wanted to tell him I was going to stay. To say I was definitely in if a lighted bouncing ball can get rid of a demon as creepy as the Evoca. However, something told me it wasn't the light which had scared the Evoca away. The ball had to have been a distraction. Demons looked nasty. I had seen a few before tonight. They were monsters. There was no way it was always so easy. If it was, every random kid with glow-in-the-dark shoes and a cult-classic mentality would be out after dark trying it.

The night flew by. None of the demons were deemed a threat by Jordan after the Evoca, and I fell more in hate with the idea of leaving. I had always been the kid who sat in the front row, hand raised at every question, and a grin on my face. Jordan was the type of guy who would have sat in the back of class sleeping and have aced every test just to spite the teachers. Kids like me—the dorky, lanky, not socially brave kind—were inexplicably drawn to people like Jordan. His coming with magic made it impossible to get away. Rattling off different facts about demons in the rough timber of his voice, he sat back in his chair. When night still lingered, dawn only an hour or two away, Jordan fell silent.

He turned to me, and I knew what he was going to ask before his lips even moved. "Have you made your decision?"

"I can't leave now. There's too much I want to know." I grinned, and he frowned as if he was disappointed by my words. "Did I say something wrong? Do you not want me as your apprentice?"

Jordan shook his head and punctuated his denial with a flick of his wrist. "There's no going back... I'm just not sure you comprehend what you're getting into by doing this."

"I get it. Cross my heart and all." I crossed my heart with my right pointer. "You're my Yoda."

"This isn't a joke, and I'm not a Jedi. You put your soul on the line when you sign up for this. Think a little before you jump into this. You don't owe anyone," Jordan retorted.

I looked back onto the street trying to think of a reply to convince him, but I failed. There was so much I wanted to learn.

So much he could teach me, and if he honestly didn't get he was my freaking Yoda, I didn't know what would work. This wasn't me being a know-it-all. Not a single word in my vocabulary could describe what I wanted. I wanted to know, and Jordan was a walking encyclopedia of demons and magic. He knew my dad. Even if there was nothing else, the last part would have been enough.

Magic had been my one and only. When we moved from apartment to apartment, I still had magic. My mom often worked late shifts. Who babysat me? Magic. The doors were locked, and I had been king of the one bedroom castle, then two-bedroom when she got her current job. It was the only secret I had, and if I couldn't learn, I was sure it would consume me.

In my mind, I saw my father. Not the real one, just the image I had made in lieu of any pictures. He smiled with my smile and told me to go for it. Magic was all I had from him. It was all I would ever have from him, and I refused to give it up. I also refused to risk my soul being consumed by keeping my magic without hunting demons. My dad had hunted demons. The only way I'd ever be like him and know him beyond the random side note of the few moments he was in my mother's life was to become a hunter. There was no way Jordan could understand the type of feeling though. He would just laugh, but I felt lying to him would be worse.

"My dad protected the world from those things." I took a deep breath. "I couldn't think of him and feel right calling myself his son if I didn't do this."

The features of Jordan's face contorted into a weird expression. I knew what it was because my mother used to get it all the time, but I hadn't seen anybody else look at me the same way before. There was an odd mix of disappointment and frustration on his face. It wasn't entirely aimed at me. If it was anything like my mom, some of it was at himself, though I had no idea why. Maybe he was just disappointed he had offered to take an idiot like me on as his apprentice.

"Your father could be dead for all you know. Do you even remember what he looks like?" He sighed, frowning. "He could have gone rogue. He might have gone nuclear and been taken for a void," Jordan said in a tone which felt as if he was letting me down gently and asking at the same time. I knew he was right, but it hadn't mattered before, and it didn't matter then.

"He was probably white," I offered.

He rolled his eyes. "You know what I mean, Jon."

"Sometimes you just have to believe even when things don't seem real or rational. You just have to be determined sometimes to believe in the things worth believing in or else you'd go insane." I shrugged.

Jordan smiled at me. I must have done something right. "Your training hasn't begun, so you should be fine once you leave. Dawn's about two hours away." He glanced at his wrist-watch. "It's almost five. You should be fine heading out now. Get some sleep and come back here tomorrow."

"Okay, what time?" I asked standing up and stretching out my legs. My left tingled from being in the same position for too many hours.

"Around two o'clock. The shop closes then, and I can teach you on the job," he explained.

As we walked down the steps, I asked, "So what's the job?"

He swung a leg over his motorcycle, putting his helmet on before answering me. "There's a group of rogues running around. Whenever you get a few in the same place, demons start to congregate around them. It's likely they're planning a summoning."

"Rogues are magic users gone bad. So how do we stop them?"

Jordan chuckled like I had made a joke. Without answering my question, he revved his bike and flew away down the street leaving me to walk back to campus in the early hours of the morning.

Four

On Sunday morning, the dining hall was a ghost town. There were random tables filled with sports teams grabbing something before morning practice or after even earlier morning practice, but things would stay dead until around eleven, so at nine-fifty in the morning I was sitting staring down at the waffle maker wondering if waffles were an appropriate meal for one's first day of magic training. Part of me still thought I was going loony bin crazy, but the excitement from the rest of me didn't give two shakes.

I was going to start learning about magic, and the paranoid part then pointed out how odd it was to not only find another person like me but find out the guy grew up with my dad. There was lucky, and there was too good to be true, yet if things were like they sounded, the magic community was not nearly as large as most fantasy novels and TV shows had told me, which was kind of disappointing. I couldn't even begin to go into detail about how much I would have loved to go to Diagon Alley or whatever American equivalent.

Eventually, my stomach spoke, and I heeded its sage advice by getting bacon from the bar and crumbling it into two waffles about the size of my face. They were an appropriate breakfast for a magical day, especially when smothered in maple syrup. Right as the crowds lined up swiping their cards to fill their zombie-like hunger, I absconded through campus and across the street to one of the more disturbing factoids of Rochester student life: the Mt.

Hope Cemetery. The cemetery was gigantic and even bigger than the main campus. If I wanted to get anywhere outside the campus eastward or north fast, Mt. Hope was the best hope. This time, I headed northeast through the park toward Benton Street. The book shop was off toward the end of Diem.

Mt. Hope was what I liked to call a necropolis. Technically, everyone should consider it among the ranks of a city of the dead; however, not a lot of people knew the wonderful word: necropolis. It made me smile every time I thought of it and rolled right off the tongue when said. There were stones from hundreds of years ago, the sort of fixtures in a Poe piece though there were more modern sections as well. Walking through the necropolis, I could watch the subtle movement through different periods of time reflect across the stones. From more grandiose mausoleums and dramatic headstones in the late eighteen hundreds and early nineteen hundreds, they shifted to more cleanly cut toward the present.

One of my old teachers back in high school had been obsessed with graveyards. Every class he held, no matter the subject, suffered through the same montage of gravestone photographs and close-up shots of epitaphs ranging from the simple RIP and date to threatening quotes like this one grave which said, "We hope he has gone to rest." Those kinds always had me feeling slightly threatened, like one day the guy would get sick of trying to sleep and would get up in a huff about his insomnia. But hey, in a world where I could control fire with a thought, zombies weren't too farfetched.

Getting to Jordan's shop before two o'clock wasn't the problem. Arriving at twelve forty-three became the issue. Once again, the glass in the window panes blended in with the glass in the buildings surrounding it. I felt a bit idiotic, but I stood in front of the bay window and leaned back and forth catching a glimpse of Jordan's motorcycle parked in the alley before finally making the move up the stairs. Taking hold of the cheeky little doorknob, I opened the door, letting the ring of the angel bell call out sharply over the whole store. Jordan leaned behind the counter with his hands braced against the edge. His glasses slid down his nose and his eyes were narrowed.

There was only one customer standing opposite to Jordan in jeans and a black shirt. The customer had brown, almost black, buzzed hair, and I couldn't see the rest of his face from the doorway, but there was something a bit strange about him. He wore black toe-shoes and drummed his toes against the wood floors. The shoes and his fidgeting weren't unusual, but the whole package rattled me a bit more than I ought to have let it. Stuffing my hands into my jean pockets, I hunched my shoulders trying to not stick out like a big bumbling moose. Frankly, it didn't matter considering the man didn't turn to look, and Jordan didn't either. I went back to the shelf with Strider's book and opened the closest one on the top shelf to the middle. My eyes flickered between the words on the page and the two of them.

"There won't be time," the man was saying. His voice was a bit deeper than my own and rose at the end of every breath. "There has to be at least five, or what they want won't work, but there isn't five—there's four. It means they'll be looking for a fifth unless they don't want to play it safe, which is possible. Then they might summon someone a bit too big, and the whole affair will end there."

"And who are they thinking of indebting?" Jordan's voice was less hoarse than before but still gravelly.

The man shifted. Multicolored eyes snapped up to stare me down. Gray and brown swirled in and out before settling in navy rings. Black scruff clung about his jaw and navy blue metal framed glasses perched on the straight bridge of his nose. A scar in the shape of a skull sat on his right cheek so perfectly I couldn't help but think it had been placed there on purpose. Realizing I was staring, I quickly looked back down at the book and caught the line, *True evil never falters.*

"He's fine," Jordan told him, and the man shifted on his toes to face Jordan once more.

"Mammon," the man said. "And he knows they want it too."

The name circled around my head like the punch line to a bad joke. I remembered who Mammon was. Indifferent and dangerous and born in Hell—not the sort of monster anyone

wanted trolling around their city. The image of those sharp edges
and overly smooth, near-faceless phantom clawing its way out of
the psychic woman from the old Keanu Reeves movie enveloped
my mind. From the huff of disappointment from Jordan, he had
some idea what I was thinking.

"I understand the situation, George." Jordan crossed his
arms with a slight smirk.

George—a rather plain name for a not so plain man—
grumbled, "This isn't the best time to be taking an apprentice."
Jordan shrugged like what George had said wasn't terribly
important. Unimpressed by Jordan's nonchalant attitude, he
turned to me. "Warlock?" I didn't know what to say in response.
"You're a warlock. Not a wizard—no training. You're not even
naturally disciplined. Played a sport? Exercise? Languages? You
aren't prepared to deal with a group of corrupted magic users,
especially not two mages, a psychic, and a warlock. All in all, one
out of four you have a chance to get the jump on if you were
running on pure instinct."

"While you're spooking him, might as well tell him the psychic is a rune master with a collection of living tattoos," Jordan
dryly noted pulling a brown leather jacket over his gray T-shirt.

I had no idea what I was supposed to say in response to either of those comments. The idea of living tattoos was cool;
however, having some oriental stylized tiger coming after me
wasn't appealing. Maybe I would get lucky and all the psychic
would have tattooed were flowers. Yeah, even I read the thought
as overly optimistic.

George turned and pulled a rectangular box, which was a bit
bigger than a set of playing cards, from his pocket. He set it down
on the counter between them.

"Play smarter."

Jordan smirked. "Not harder." He placed his hand on the
other side of the box. They nodded at each other once, and then
George turned and left with only the jingle of the ringer acknowledging his absence.

Putting the book back on the shelf, I walked briskly to the
counter. "Living tattoos?"

"Well, if you see any slightly two-dimensional animals or people running around, run," Jordan informed me. "Not much else to say about her."

The fact he didn't get it made me repeat the question. "Living tattoos?"

He hummed a jaunty tune and mumbled something about a woman named Lydia before retorting, "We'll deal when we come to it. If they're working toward a contract with a major demon like Mammon, she won't be wasting her energy on her tattoos. Runes or not, they still take more power than she can afford until they find a fifth to stabilize their circle."

"Pentagram," I offered, and he shook his head.

"Pentagon if you must. More points, more users, less effort, less risk." He snorted. "Ideally. Demons don't generally do low risk though, especially not Mammon."

Glancing down, my eyes landed on the box George had left. It was a container of tarot cards, or so the gold writing on the front said. I reached forward to pick them up, but Jordan slid them away and into a brown bag on a stool behind the counter I hadn't seen there last night.

"What did he mean about Mammon being aware? Does it mean he'll come on his own?" I asked.

Jordan frowned for a moment then sighed. "They wouldn't make the deal if he goes to them. He'll pretend he hasn't caught wind and wait for the summons while putting traps around the city, so when they do summon him, things will go wrong. If we run into him now, he won't be under their command which means he isn't the enemy yet for the sake of this job. It also means he won't likely attack any magic user in the city directly. He will, however, try to influence the choice of their fifth. If even one member of the summoning twists a line, the entire group is left vulnerable."

"Why would they bother summoning a demon? They have magic," I pointed out. "What do they need him for?"

"To be frank, I haven't a clue. At the close of an apprenticeship, apprentices summon and obliterate a low level demon. It's called the First Summoning. For most, the experience is chilling enough they don't ever want to do it again. When people go rogue, it's normally magicians and psychics. The other three categories normally have the capacity to get what they want and will get lazy before getting corrupted. This group has been building for years," he said.

"Building?" I considered for a minute. "Like a job, right? One person pulling in help?"

"If you want to think of it in those terms, go ahead. The rogue who instigates a summoning circle is the originator. Ours is a seventy-five-year-old mage by the name of Giuseppe—went south in about '05 and found the warlock, Madrid, in '09 when she turned fifteen along with her aunt, Rio." He shuffled through some papers pulling out an ad for palm readings with a rather pretty though bored looking woman. "Rio was a renowned psychic who had gone rogue back in the eighties when she, herself, was in her teens. Some more years and tattoos later, the three recently acquired a fourth member: Henry Blake—mage, twenty-eight, recently widowed."

Four super powerful magic users who were all way more trained than I was, and Jordan thought it was just the best idea to go up against them like they were no real problem. George had been nervous. He had said I was a warlock, but obviously the level wasn't good enough in the face of those four. I got Jordan was probably a wizard, but there were still two mages and a warlock he'd have to take out on his own. It all meant we were at a clear disadvantage. Screwed one might even say.

"How exactly did people not think of them a threat when there were just three to deal with?"

Jordan scratched at the stubble at his jaw line. While the rest of his hair was white, the stubble looked black. "They didn't summon demons. All three ran from authorities, but they didn't go bad. They just ran without hurting anyone, which is extremely uncommon. For a while, people thought Giuseppe was working under the Daughters to get Madrid back into the fold and out of the influence of her aunt. With Henry Blake in the mix, there isn't much use pretending they aren't aiming for a higher level summoning, and with Blake, we know what they all have in common."

"Magic?" The level of sarcasm needed to pull the word off was not within my repertoire, but it was worth the glower I got in response.

"Loss. Giuseppe's wife was a normal—no magic—who had dementia with additional loss of motor function due to damage to her nervous system caused by a demon coming after Giuseppe. She's currently in a hospice center in Toronto. Madrid lost both her parents and was taken in by Rio who lost her husband and three-month-old son to a rogue when the Daughters requested her aid in finding him..." He trailed off, and I nodded.

"And Blake just lost his wife," I filled in. "Which means we're looking for a fifth in this city who has suffered a loss, but what does it mean regarding what they want to do? A demon can't bring someone back from the dead, right?"

"Demons can do some extraordinary things. Mammon could heal Giuseppe's wife if he wanted to by voiding the illness from her." Jordan's brows knotted. He paused, gazing off, then shrugged. "As for the dead, Mammon could only bring them back, in theory, if their souls had collapsed and were consumed. He could find the demon, tear apart its void, and bring them back if they hadn't been dead for an extended period of time. Honestly, Blake's the only one with a chance. His wife died about a month ago, but as far as I know she'd been an avid hunter until the end."

I scrunched my nose in disgust. "Void her illness? Why can't Giuseppe do it? Or why can't the group just combine their powers and do it themselves? Why do they need a demon?"

"We can't heal others." He was lying. I didn't know how I knew, but some part of me knew what he was saying was a half-truth. I didn't have the courage to argue the point yet.

"But demons can?"

"They void—reversing, degrading, destroying—and yes, includes illnesses. If they had any good will left in them, they could be an immeasurable amount of help," Jordan said.

"So..." I glanced at my watch. It was still only one-twenty, but I was getting edgy. "Why don't you close up shop early and we can get this show on the road?"

Shaking his head, Jordan gestured to the table and chairs by the bay window. "Relax and read a book. Do your homework. I made a deal with the owner of this shop that I would maintain its schedule while he was on vacation in exchange for room and board. You can wait forty minutes."

"Come on." I slouched against the counter. "No one's here! You could at least get my training started!"

He pointed to the chair, and when I trudged over, I noticed a thin book on the table labeled, *The Journal of Madeline Graham*. Underneath in the subtitle, silver words curled like smoke stating, *A Tale of A Sold Soul*. I flipped the book to the back, looking for a description or something, but all there was on the back cover was a picture of this girl who looked like she was barely old enough to attend high school let alone actually have thoughts deep enough to put in a book. I glanced over at Jordan who had returned to his position behind the desk. He had the box of tarot cards out again and had set it upon the counter. He stared at it like it was some sort of bomb ticking away and about to explode. Jordan reached forward and lifted the top, but he ultimately glanced up at me after a few seconds.

"Read." He gestured with the top of the box, and I could hear him set the piece down on the table as I did so.

The book itself wasn't horrible. There was some stretch to the prose giving away the author's age—sixteen years old. When she finished the book though it was published posthumously by her father. However, the story itself sucked me in. The main character was a werewolf, but not the kind who instinctively fell in love with their soulmate. This was a werewolf resulting from something a bit more in line with Jordan's reality and the mythology I was more comfortable with—a curse. The girl in the book, Madeline Graham, hadn't even been born yet when her mother got into a stir of bad luck resulting in a precarious position where she made a deal with a demon. Except, she wasn't the only soul in her body, but she was the only soul within the body with the capacity for conscious decision; needless to say, Madeline was born with her soul already promised. She'd been saved from consumption by her father cutting her free from her mother as her mother was consumed by the demon leaving her marked and hunted.

This wasn't the hairy kind of lupine curse, but one of uncontrollable rages and inhuman strength tied to the waning and waxing of the moon. The end was less than stellar. I was always the happy ending sort, and Madeline ended up dead at seventeen, having been exhausted by her constant struggles against the demons who whispered in her ears. Other magic users claimed she was more the daughter of the demon who dealt for her mother's soul than the father who had endlessly done his best to protect her. It was a novella more than a book with only five chapters of about one hundred pages.

First chapter covered her mother's deal and her father saving her life. Second, third, and fourth chapters covered her life running with her father—Louis, pronounced the French way. He used up every last favor owed to him to keep her alive while they made jarring comments behind his back to his daughter saying she never had a soul. Toward the end of four, her father had spent all he had creating a huge glass house with a forest built within to protect her while giving her the stars she craved.

The fifth and final chapter encompassed her death. There was a buildup in each chapter with her capacity to rationalize her own emotions failing, while the voices plaguing her and sending her into animalistic rages grew stronger. The final page of the fifth was a short poem, and while there was nothing actually discussing her planning her death, there was a rather intricate tombstone pictured. The base was square with the names and dates, but on top was a young girl in a Victorian dress passing through a looking glass. I had no idea what exactly I was supposed to learn reading this.

> *Where must I go? From where have I come?*
> *I understood the premise*
> *The cat was a menace*
> *With relief, I will finally succumb*
>
> *Dad, I apologize for tonight*
> *You did your best*

For this, I was blessed
Despite the weight of mother's blight

I tried to overcome
But now I am undone

The poem was rather puerile, especially in rhyme scheme and basic vocabulary, but beyond anything else I had no idea if it was good or not. I always understood the laws of writing, yet couldn't appreciate the context. Probably ought to have just said good. It had been her note. Her father wrote a short paragraph barely two sentences long explaining. She had committed suicide in her glass house with a scarf made into a necklace tied to the limb of a tree. I turned around, and Jordan was watching me carefully.

"You done?" he asked and gestured at the clock. It was fifteen past two.

Abandoning the book and whatever I was supposed to get out of it on the table, I stood up stretching to touch the relatively low ceiling of the store. "What exactly are we doing today?"

Jordan flicked off the lights and held the door open, waiting to speak until I passed through. "Today, I have to interview a few suspected possible fifths. We need a read about who is going to get picked."

Shutting the door behind us, Jordan didn't even take out a key or anything. He just unhooked the angel ringer and closed the door. The ram's skull was back with those nasty, glittering eyes looking like it was enjoying a good sunning with the early Sunday closing. Jumping down from the top set to the street, I stuck my hands in my sweatshirt pocket turning around to face Jordan who had his own hands in his leather jacket pockets. In comparison to his rather suave style, I was the epitome of a college student, non-chic despite my jeans actually fitting.

"So, how's this going to help my training?" I asked when we had set a pace walking down the street.

"One—you get some Rochester connections with a clear idea of who you can trust and who you can't. Two—you'll get the firsthand experience of magic to magic interactions. Third." He stopped glancing at me. "Shields. A good shield is hard to find. Most magic users spend their time learning how to fight demons which means learning indirect methods of influence. A flame started by magic isn't useful against demons, but manipulated flame started by traditional forces can be. Direct methods are generally only taught by the Daughters or Sons, which is a mistake."

"Hold up, why can't I just burn up a demon?" This whole direct versus indirect methods seemed a little overly complex.

"Magic has a mind of its own, and it has no qualm against hurting humans, magic or not, but demons are on its side. Same end goal." Jordan pointed at me then downwards. "Shields."

"Yeah, okay, shields," I said, and we continued walking.

"What do you think of when you think of protection?"

The first thing to pop into my head was something so far from our conversation I didn't even bother mentioning it; the second was not much better. "A shield."

I didn't have to look at Jordan to know he was looking at me like I was an idiot. I understood my brain worked a little bit too literally. Thankfully, he skipped over saying anything at least. "Then keep the sort of image in mind and realize whatever you imagine will project the limits whether it's a wooden shield only covering your torso or the upper curve of a medieval English shield."

"Maybe a hazmat suit would be better," I joked.

"Probably would be," Jordan retorted. "I generally go for a bomb disposal suit."

When he was talking, a shimmer encircled him. He was surrounded by a gray, near-invisible aura the shape of giant armor before expanding to form a castle around his body. The force moved outwards, and when it hit me, I almost fell over only to have it absorb me before the shield popped like a bubble. The entire time he had kept walking down the street like nothing was going on, and the few scattered other people didn't act like they noticed a thing. Instead of being one of those smart students who asks questions, I decided the best idea would be to directly attempt what I had seen. A wisp rolled off of me like heat rising from the pavement in the evening. More and more gathered, curling around me like a steam cloud.

Jordan laughed swatting the wisps. "I keep forgetting you've never been trained."

"You said it was just will," I retorted, trying harder. The wisps formed a shimmer around me, but still wavered.

"Don't think about it like you saw it. Think about what you want. Don't try to rationalize whether it is vapors or auras or whatever. Think shield." Jordan obviously had never had a student before because it was the worst advice I'd ever heard. Regardless, I have always prided myself on my capacity to learn even from the most indiscernible teachers.

I imagined a shield. I didn't try to think about a biohazard suit or some sort of bullet proof vest. I thought about what it felt like to be on the receiving end of a charge. Fights had never been my thing. People normally liked me fine even if I was a bit geeky or a bit too whatever to be good friends with, so imaging a need for a defense was the best I could do. More wisps appeared a bit clearer and a bit more solid than the first, but they weren't what they needed to be. Jordan, the smug, self-important jerk, watched me out of the corner of his eye with the same smirk on his face.

"It's not funny. Shouldn't this be easier?" I grumbled shoving my hands into my pockets and glaring down at the ground because its actual existence offended me at the moment.

Jordan patted me on the shoulder. "If you could do a shield easily, I would be rather concerned about your upbringing. Magic is built on instinct. If you had preciously needed a shield, you'd know how to do it already."

"I didn't need to know how to move water or make fire into shapes, but I can do it," I pointed out only to earn another laugh. "Come on, it has to be useful somehow."

"I'm sure it will come in handy," he assured me. "But it was purely entertainment. There's a rather high chance you also channel your magic to run faster, jump higher, climb things easier, and so forth."

"Which would be helpful."

"Athletic desire—physical result: it's just about wanting something bad enough or being desperate enough," Jordan said before frowning up at a group of apartment buildings across the street from us.

While he stared like a sort of awkward Jedi, I tried to think about even one moment in my life where I needed protection I couldn't get anywhere else. I had been pretty lucky all things considered. I had, however, read plenty of books and seen numerous shows and movies wherein the characters struggled to survive. Surely I could simply imagine an army of salt and pepper shakers with toilet plungers and whisks for hands chasing me down. Maybe they were wood, and I was the only defense we had. A weight settled on my arm, and there it was—a medieval shield because my brain didn't practice logic.

"How do I make it bigger?" It was heavy like actual metal, which was sort of concerning.

Jordan grabbed the edges and stretched it out to a sort of Spartan defense going from my knees to above my head. He hummed softly then let go. I was barely able to adjust to the new weight in time. I didn't have to even think twice, and the shield was light again. Jordan sighed looking at the shrunken force, so I expanded it once more.

"You're going to have to practice," Jordan informed me turning back to look at the apartment building. "Our first possible fifth is Prudence Hail."

"What?" I continued to play with the size of the shield, but the name caught my attention.

"She's an eighty-three-year-old woman who has two cats. She is blind from a childhood accident." The way he said the word made me certain it wasn't actually an accident.

"She's old. Why is she on the list?"

Jordan glanced at me with narrowed eyed, raised eyebrow look. "She's eighty-three not dead."

"She's close enough. Why would she want to risk it for Mammon? I mean, seriously, Prudence?" I shook my arm letting the shield drop. "She sounds like a puritanical nightmare."

Shrugging, Jordan crossed the street without looking both

ways, and as a result, numerous cars honked as he walked casually through. "You're about right."

I waved a hand in apology to the cars. "Then why is she on the list?"

Jordan didn't have to give me a look for me to realize my mistake. I knew the moment I said it the reason she was on the list was because she was a bit too solid in her way of thinking. It seemed to happen to people. They were good, but then the lines got too inflexible, and the importance of the nuances was lost, meaning the reality of human life was lost. He pressed the buzzer and waited. When the temperature dropped, I didn't think much of it considering it was still early enough in spring for Rochester to decide it wasn't completely finished with winter. Then the wind buzzed, and a voice like the crypt keeper came over the system.

"What do *you* want?"

Jordan leaned forward. "Just to talk, Prudence."

"No."

The intercom clicked and then shut off completely. The miniature cold front left promptly around the same time. Jordan pressed the button a second time and waited. The same chill ran through my bones, followed by the same humming feeling ticking against my brain, leaving me antsy.

The same grave voice came. "I said no."

"We need to talk, Prudence, or I'm going to report your location and lack of cooperation with the Sisters," he said casually. The underlying threat balanced in a procedural tone which would have pissed anyone off. Still, there was something ominous about the threat.

"We're talking right now, wretch! Say your piece and get you gone." It was like listening to one of those early Sunday morning televangelists doing some sort of exorcism.

Jordan sighed, rubbing the bridge of his nose with his right forefinger and thumb. "Prudence—has anyone else come to visit recently?"

"My visitors are none of your business."

"Have you seen Giuseppe? Henry Blake? Either Rio or Madrid of the Peruvian Alvarez house?" He asked the question slowly and cautiously, but she listened without interrupting.

"Giuseppe? Sounds like a dirty Italian—I don't take kindly to those people," Prudence grumbled. "Those backwards south-types too! Blake?" she repeated the name and seemed to chew the word apart. "He's been 'round."

Turning from the intercom, Jordan ran his hand against the door. "Are you going to let us in, Prudence?" He pushed me gently out of the way back down the stairs, and as we reached the bottom, a woman holding a small child went up and opened the door. With a twist of wind, Jordan caught the edge and held it open. We walked into the building, and as the door closed behind us, Prudence's voice resonated in the empty space we left behind.

"Why would I let you and the half-blood in?"

Five

The building was plain and relatively clean, which was a step up from the hall of my dormitory, yet there was this dank smell hanging around the entrance to the third floor. The smell lessened, then grew again around apartment 310 until it was almost overpowering at Hail's apartment, 321. The number one was a bit crooked. The three had rust covering the upper curve. Around the doorway, there was a small square of rug grayer than the surrounding flooring. The walls were plain, but the section of ceiling directly above the square was burnt. Glancing back down at the rug, I shuffled my foot. Yep, it was dust-a-la-demon-flambé.

Jordan knocked twice, and the small peephole clicked as it was opened from the inside. One large blue eye glowered out at us like the evil eye incarnate, or maybe I couldn't tell either way because peepholes weren't big enough. Plus, she was blind, so there wouldn't have been a reason for her to look through the peephole. Either way, the intensity of loathing was dropped on us regardless of whether or not the aforementioned optic sphere was visible. I, however, stood by my assertion the nasty, cataract covered, blue eye was visible like some menace on a spell book bound in human flesh like a 90s Halloween special.

"Go away."

"They are looking for a fifth, Prudence. We need to speak or I have to contact the Sisters," he informed her. Maybe I was just getting a bit too into my head, but the temperature felt warmer than it had a moment ago. "I'm on my third strike. I can't exactly not fulfill this hunt."

"Wow, double negatives. I can feel her fighting the tempta-tion to open her house to us." Maybe it was a bit snarky, but I could feel the demon dust getting into my shoes.

The door burst open to show a tall woman with long thin limbs and a gaunt face. Her silver hair was streaked with black and down to her waist in a tight braid, swinging behind her like a whip. She had thick eyebrows which fell heavily over her eyes in a permanent scowl. A long, brown skirt fell from her waist to her feet where she had slipped on those popular plush boots in beige. Her cream shirt was covered by a thickly knitted, gray cardigan and an even larger brown shawl she had wrapped about her shoulders. Long, gnarled fingers held the two ends of the shawl where they crossed against her chest. Ovular glasses like the ones from any pharmacy in plain black plastic sat upon her narrow nose and reassured me I had, in fact, seen her terribly blue eye from the other side of the door.

"Are those words any way to talk to your master?" She spoke with a testing tone. The words were dry and held out at the end while she brought her chin to her chest and considered me.

Jordan's shoulders hadn't seemed tense, yet when he ex-haled, they sank just enough to reveal he had been. He smiled warmly at this cantankerous old woman. "Prudence, may we come in for tea?"

"Are you going to just let the boy get away with such a smart mouthed comment? He's going to get himself killed if he goes around saying what he wants without any little bit of anything to back up such brashness." She shook her head and sniffed the air like she could smell me getting roasted already. "In my day, apprentices respected those who were willing to teach them."

"He's young—this is his first day." Jordan shrugged, and Prudence stepped out of the way to make room for us to enter.

"Sparing the rod won't keep him any safer," Prudence sug-gested—again far more gently than she had over the intercom. The strange personality shift was throwing me. "Fine, fine—come in."

Jordan bowed his head. At first, I thought he was nodding in agreement, but he lowered his gaze and sidestepped into the apartment without further comment on whether or not I needed 'the rod.' I, in my own turn passing through, was cornered by the invisible though heavy weight of her gaze shifting from exhausted school matron to vicious recluse. I wasn't buying the blind routine.

"Thank you?" I ventured uncertain what exactly she wanted from me.

She shook her head saying, "Just another foolish boy thinking he can own the world."

"He thinks he's a superhero," Jordan called from within the apartment.

He was seated on an old-fashioned sofa with a single cushion and four ornate wooden legs. The back and arms were curved outwards. The only time I had seen one of those types of Victorian couches was at my grandparents' house the one Christmas we were invited to dinner. The rug was a floral pattern; I was pretty sure the red blobs were meant to be roses. Fake daisies filled random cups and vases around the well-sized main room. Another glass vase sat upon the kitchen table in the blindingly white kitchen.

"Not a superhero," I grumbled as she shut the door behind me. Jordan raised an eyebrow and I folded. "Sidekick."

His face fell into his hand, and he shook his head, refusing to look at me while Prudence slipped around me with a grimace. "In your own life? Oh, you're a bit of an odd duck, aren't you?"

I sat down in a wooden rocking chair beside a towering basket of yarn only to be shooed away over to the couch where Jordan was seated. Prudence brushed off her shirt and placed the shawl over the back of the rocker before she reached over and picked up what looked to be the beginnings of another cardigan—this time a dark navy—from the basket. Sitting down, she returned to her knitting and let the apartment fall into silence when I failed to come up with a proper response to her utterly accurate assessment.

"Prudence, why did Blake meet with you?" Jordan opened up the floor to conversation while I attempted to not appear completely out of place.

"He wanted to say hello," she said. "He's such a sweet young man. Shame about Elise."

"Did he tell you why he's in town?" Jordan pressed.

Prudence scoffed. "Mammon! The wretched bull-headed boy thinks Elise can be pulled back from the other side. Giuseppe has him all tangled up. Told him she wasn't where Mammon could go, but he's—well..." She smirked deviously. "He's quite like you, Jordan. Thinks he can see the big picture. Of course, he doesn't understand there are some things better left to those capable of actually seeing it."

"Did he—"

Prudence cut him off with a glower. "Did he what? Did he ask me to join them? Am I the fifth? Is that where we're going with this? You and I both know the only thing left to offer me is an escape from this infirmity. Always cold, blind, tired in aches I never had—a demon may be able to void age as well as any other wound, but we both know helping wouldn't be what Mammon would do."

Her fingers didn't move like they were arthritic, twisting around the knitting needles and manipulating the chords of yarn. The thought—barely a second long—was followed by an all-consuming mixture of fear and disbelief. The idea demons could remove disease using their void was one thing, but even the suggestion they could reverse aging left me sick. Demons had a lot of fantasy abilities which would have fictionally either put them into the annoying-person-everyone-dies-for category—which was completely off from the point—or the jerk-everyone-else-died-protecting—as long as we didn't get too religious there. In every game I had played on every gaming console my friends had, the healers were the guys who were a one-per-group-at-least require-ment. Demons weren't the same though. They didn't give a crap if other people died, and the fact they could save countless lives was beyond insane.

Jordan rested a hand on my shoulder pulling me out of my head when he said, "You didn't answer the question, Prudence."

"You didn't ask it."

"Did he ask you to join them? And did you agree?"

"Yes and no, in the same order."

Jordan nodded, taking his hand from my shoulder. "And do you plan on joining them?"

"Plan to? No, I'm close enough to the end of this race I can almost taste the winner's circle," she said sounding a bit more like the woman who had grouched over the intercom.

"All right."

Her eyes narrowed. "Of course, it's all right. It's a sight more than most in my situation would do, mind you. Now, you better put in a good word with those higher up friends of yours. I don't want to see anybody on my doorstep unless they're asking me where to hunt you."

"Certainly." Jordan stood. "Pleasure as always, Prudence."

The door swung open while Prudence continued to knit. "Pleasure doesn't describe it. Don't forget the half-breed!"

The couch jumped, shoving me off, and I quickly headed toward the door. Jordan smirked. The door slammed behind us before we were completely out, leaving a clear message of how little she wanted a return visit. Sticking my hands in my pockets, I followed Jordan back out of the building, not bringing up the questions hovering around my head. The biggest part of me wanted to scream and rant about the whole half-breed and half-blood part. I had kind of hoped the magical community didn't have those prejudices. Real life didn't have awesome schools and owls as pets, so there was no reason it had to have the same blood-drawn lines. Magic was such a great big pile of not-good it made it difficult to swallow another bitter pill.

It wasn't the first time someone looked at me funny because of my parents. I knew she wasn't able to tell who my mom was, though I had gotten plenty of looks when I went anywhere with her. My mom had this tightly-coiled, dark brown hair and sort of dark caramel complexion with my grandfather's hazel eyes. Besides the eyes, I didn't look like her side of the family at all. Everyone was tall, but my nose was a bit narrower. I knew what it was like to be looked at sideways. People thought my mom couldn't be my real mom. When they realized she was, some would get a look of uncertainty especially if they knew my dad wasn't around, and those types of people always knew.

"It was the magic right?" I asked when I couldn't keep it in anymore. Jordan glanced at me in confusion. "She was calling me half-breed because my mom doesn't have magic."

He frowned. "Yeah."

I nodded glaring at the ground. "Okay, it's—fine."

The weight of his gaze followed me until he said, "You're better off with a mortal parent. The less magic you have, the less likely you are to be damned."

"Great," I grumbled, hunching my shoulders. I never knew why, but those sorts of situations always left me feeling ungainly.

"Jon."

"Don't—my mom's kind of already covered all the rationalizations. This isn't the first time someone thought of me as a half-breed. At least she had the decency to say it to my face," I said.

Jordan let the subject drop and led us further into the city. I wasn't certain he had any idea where we were headed when he stopped at a street corner. He glanced in one direction and squinted like he was zooming in on the other side of town. When his eyes relaxed, he turned his attention in the opposite direction. Stretching his neck—a few pops and cracks had me a bit twitchy—Jordan turned to me with a sigh.

"Hunt or part ways?" he said.

"More details?" I asked in return, not exactly sure what he was trying to get at.

Jordan pointed across the street. "There's an old score I've got to settle over on the other side of the city. You can come—staying back and keeping quiet—or you can go home and we'll meet up once I have another possible fifth."

"I thought you researched before we met up?" Despite my saying this, I was already trying to see the old score. It had to be a demon. "If Prudence is it, why didn't we just take her out?"

"People pass this area all the time. It wouldn't be too much of a stretch to assume they've planned a meeting rather than they are going to a meeting. Magic users aren't fond of doing summoning in cities they like," he explained, and I understood the premise but bristled at the idea Giuseppe had no problem leveling Rochester if it came to it. "At least two other hunters are headed this way—Deacon Sullivan and Maxwell Ericson."

"So—why don't we just meet them today?"

He sighed rubbing the bridge of his nose. "Neither is currently here."

"We could drive. You have a motorcycle," I pointed out. I had always wanted to ride on a motorcycle. My mom always thought it was too dangerous. Considering she worked in forensics recreating motor vehicle accidents, I thought she was kind of bias.

"I'd rather not." Jordan looked away from me, watching a city bus come to a haltering stop at the light. "Hunt or part ways?"

"Hunt."

It wasn't even a good question. I had the time, and I wasn't going to stop this crazy adventure no matter what the old coot said. I might be a sidekick now, but all the best sidekicks became heroes. Pressing the signal, Jordan leaned back waiting until the little walking man appeared before dashing across the street. I followed, excited to see where we'd end up this time. We walked almost three blocks before stopping on a more artistic side of town. Random indie stores lined the side of the street we were on, and outside a coffee shop, a homeless man in ragged clothing sat with a drunken smile upon his lips.

His eyes, a light gray, were clouded by exhaustion or drugs or who knows what. His lips were chapped and seemed white due to the skin peeling off of them. His hair was a soft red and in general disarray casting odd shadows across his upturned face. He had antique spectacles resting on the tip of his nose. They were wire frames and the glass was shaped into thin rectangles. A flush covered his already sunburned skin, and a small coffee can, the old tin kind, sat at his side. Scrawled in black sharpie were the words, "Poetry for Your Soul."

He seemed completely normal, and if I had any money, I might have given him some if it weren't for the whole soul-wanting business. When we reached him, a group of young women in their teens were gathered around him. They were giggling as girls were ought to do, and they glanced between each other conspiratorially. Jordan's pace slowed from a brisk walk to a leisurely pace, though any onlooker wouldn't have been able to see the difference in the way he walked. He always looked like he was gliding across the world, or maybe just standing still as it flew by him.

"Fair ladies." The man's smile was open, and it made me smile even from a bit off. "You asked for a poem and yet gave me some change instead of your soul. Whatever am I to do with this?" He held up a handful of nickels, dimes, and pennies with a few quarters before letting it fall between his fingers and back into the can. "I suppose it is for the best; I should not hunt in the Devil's territory."

"Where's our poem?" One of them sneered while the others laughed behind false coy hands.

"Infantile child, challenging years with disdain and contempt / Fearless in a mind lying within the hands of a merciless god / Thinking kindly of yourself, but you are nothing more / than a doll talking without speaking / hears, without listening. Infantile child, / little girl who claims her place upon the world / without knowing what lies within it, / can you not see you are nothing / more than a blink of my eyes. / I sleep longer than you have been alive. / I have taken higher breathes than all of yours added upon each other." He lifted his head as he spoke, and when he was finished, he let out a breath slowly as if to emphasize his point as his face upturned again.

The one girl turned and stormed into the coffee shop, swearing beneath her breath. Jordan and I stopped and hung back as the rest of the girls looked at the man and chanted, almost as one, "What about me? Make a poem for me!"

The hand resting on the can after letting the coins drop pointed at one of the remaining three girls. "Here is the day which casts no shadows. / Stand forth and let your words become / the stars you gaze upon at night. / There is someone listening / to each as if it was a universe within its own. / Reach out to the hand holding yours / when darkness cast no light upon your lips." His finger stretched and pointed at another while the one turned and texted someone on her phone. "Sinister, the eyes which see. / Cold, those who are blind. / What lamb falls to the slaughter? / What love have you left behind? / Where is your taunting smile now, / oh forgotten mistress all to waste? / Could you taunt the stars for shining / because they leave your eyes disgraced?" The woman who he had been pointing to looked resigned at his words as if she refused to argue what she knew to be true of her character.

"And me?" a soft voice came from the sad eyes of the third.

The man's brows knotted, and his lips turned downwards in empathy. "Standings, arms spread /a sacrifice for you, / calling the names /of the demons / who haunted your day. / Swearing life, / swearing blood for you. / Giving everything away, / just so you might survive. /Wings like an angel's, / but blackened with soot. / Lightning makes the sky dance. / The earth trembles in fear /as the flames rise. / He died for you. / Fell into the darkness for you. / Gave his life / for you. / He died, / he lived, /all for you / until the end. /And even then, / it was all for you."

The girl's hands trembled and came before her lips which quaked as if to allow sobs to pass. Tears rolled down her pallid cheeks, and she shook her head as if it would rid her of the emotion. The man simply looked on with a light envy in his otherwise flat features. He seemed distant while appearing intrigued at the same time.

Finally, the last one's hands dropped enough her lips were visible as she whispered, "Thank you," and fled with her friends following close after her, leaving the man alone.

He stared down at his hands and said to no one, "Again, I have spoken of you with praise. This time, have I earned forgiveness for a deed for which I will never apologize?" He then bowed his head and waited. "Your voice echoes in the Absence. / It spills over the world and gives life. / Life was never known till you whispered. / Love was never known till you sang. / Your voice echoes in the highest mountains and lowest seas. / Your voice echoes in the Absence."

"Oh, Belial." Jordan shook his head as if commiserating with the man—demon, he had to be a demon. "The last one was honestly one of the worst poems you have spouted out to date.

You're getting sloppy."

To be honest, I liked it, but I wasn't bringing it up then. As we already discussed, literature critique wasn't my strong suit, and complimenting demons wasn't on my to-do list. He looked especially human. There weren't any extra limbs or creepy teeth. Compared to every demon I'd ever seen, he was perfectly human, if a bit drugged out. Plus, the level of communication put him in a category undoubtedly out of my league.

"I know. I know... oh how I comprehend. But there is little I can do," Belial replied softly. "This is the twelfth time you have passed... will you leave in the same manner or do you challenge?"

Looking at me over his shoulder, Jordan smiled. "Eashians won't attack at random like other demons. However, their idea of random and ours is a bit different." I couldn't help but tense. "It will only tempt when challenged to tempt and will only harm when challenged to harm."

"I get he's a demon, but he seems awfully—calm..." It wasn't the right word. I didn't have the right word to explain he seemed too human.

"If all demons are the remnants of fallen angels, than Eashians are the ones who shattered the least while still shattering at least a minute amount. Eashians have names," Jordan explained gesturing at Belial. "Like the Devil."

"What?" I stepped back. "I don't think I'm up for anything so powerful."

"He's not too powerful," Jordan informed me though Belial's eyebrows knotted, and he looked up at Jordan with an accusing stare. "Those who didn't shatter—the three born, Lilith, and the Devil—have the capacity to recognize names, both their own and others. Eashians don't acknowledge the other. Often they'll call you by their name," Jordan explained as he looked back at Belial. "They are also more likely to respond to a single particular emotional output than any other."

"I respond well to lust." Belial smiled, and his eyes sparkled from beneath his spectacles. "But most won't be as forthright as I am about it. I suspect it is why Belial hasn't blasted me to oblivion yet."

At first, I thought he was joking when he said Belial instead of Jordan, but the expression on his face was absolutely serious. Quickly jotting down what I had been told, I realized the sun had been up for a good long while, yet Belial was still outside.

"Why isn't Belial dead? Did he just show up?"

"No, he's been here all day." Jordan's eyes narrowed. "Possibly longer considering the amount of coins."

"The sun's setting in an hour or two—like seriously, going on four o'clock," I said glancing between Belial and Jordan. I was totally the kid who got all disappointed when facts learned in one class were disproved in the next year.

Belial sighed and looked down at his wristwatch, which was a tacky piece of plastic in the shape of Big Ben. "It isn't terribly late..."

"Eashians also have a penchant for killing themselves. Due to their emotional disconnection, they can't always feel their voids and often stay on Earth too long," Jordan told me, and I focused my eyes to see the dark nothing of Belial's void. It was about the size of a motorcycle. I had to admit I was impressed. "Belial's one of the more peaceful ones. After him, Abigor is probably the least threatening."

"I know that one!" Belial exclaimed. "He likes to sing a lot... He's the Belial pinned to revelry. All braids and no brains that one."

The street suddenly seemed to empty in a most certainly unnatural way. It was then I noticed we were not where I thought we had been. Instead of on a street corner, we were in an alley, and Belial was standing. He stretched and smiled gently at Jordan. Jordan pulled a can of hair spray out of a pocket somewhere in his jacket and his lighter out of his back pocket. Belial frowned.

"You didn't think I'd just let you win, did you?" Jordan jested with a smile, and it was the weirdest thing. The smile was more genuine than any other smile Jordan had given. He looked like he was exactly where he wanted to be, which I suppose he was.

Belial shook his head. "God has forgotten me."

Jordan didn't say a thing. He just flicked one and pushed down the other. A flame threw itself toward Belial, completely engulfing him. I was certain Belial's void would be completely gone by the time the first few minutes passed, but Jordan held tightly to both even as a light pink stained the thumb of his lighter hand. When the flame finally stopped, Jordan tossed the empty can aside. Belial was unharmed and swaying a bit on his feet as though he were drunk more than anything else. I held back a curse of bemusement and squinted to see if his void was whole. During the time I was searching for it, Jordan pulled out a bottle of lighter fluid and squirted some at Belial. I followed the line of liquid and saw the void; it was no bigger than a basketball.

"I'm insulted—I think," Belial muttered as he stared down at the line of fluid. He picked up his void and looked at it as if it had done something to him.

Jordan lit a match and tossed it. I was sure it would have hit the void, but Belial blew it out midair. "Seriously, you're going to be like this about it?" Jordan asked, and Belial glowered.

"You're trying to completely destroy me and you ask if I'm going to be like this? You are a shower, Belial!" The demon roared, and Jordan burst out laughing. Belial frowned knowing he had messed up somewhere along the line.

"You mean 'douche,'" Jordan corrected and lit another match. This time he lit two wooden things, three-inch cubes I believe, and threw one after another.

Belial jumped around dodging the blows until he took a bit of a wrong turn and stood only a foot away from Jordon. His void was still in his arms. It was dark and swirling in its emptiness. "Crap," was the last word he said as Jordan flicked the match.

The world around us exploded. There was no terror on Belial's face as he erupted into flames. It was almost a look of absolute relief. A smile pulled at his lips and tears, which the fire devoured, moistened his eyes. I expected Belial to vanish just like the other demons had. Simply poof and be gone forever. Instead, there was the sound of tearing flesh, and wings—three pairs—sprung fourth from his back. There were feathers missing, and his skin looked oddly sallow as if he were ill verging on dying. He looked straight at us. His left eye closed and sunk in as though he did not have an eye to keep it up. The remaining feathers were unlike anything I could have imagined. It was like stardust, refracted light, and a third thing so far outside of human understanding I couldn't image a single thing similar to compare. I still can't. Each feather ebbed and flowed like each was its own miniature ocean. Then Belial shattered completely, and the fire turned the light inside out and the stardust simply became soot.

Jordan stared down at the place where Belial had been with a sad sort of tilt to his head. I felt pity well up inside of me. Belial had once been an angel—a being of the greatest good imaginable. Now he was nothing but a smudge on the road. Technically, not even the smudge as the dust blew away, and there soon was no evidence he had ever existed at all. Human lives were the length of gnats in comparison to demons and angels, but after death, the memory of us could linger. Our bodies took time, years to completely erode, and our families kept us alive.

"I know it's useless, but will anyone remember Belial? Do demons mourn?" My inquiry was made slowly—cautiously because I wasn't sure I wanted an answer.

Jordan turned his back to the spot and glanced at me out of the corner of his eye. "Apparently you," he said and shoved his hands into his jacket pockets. "I don't know for sure, but I doubt any demons will mourn him."

Jordan walked off, and I quickly followed, yet it felt as though the spot loomed behind us. I had witnessed the death of a fallen angel who had been complete in all but mind. There was something utterly tragic about the affair. It was like pulling the wings off a butterfly, or more accurately, like killing a tiger. Tigers could kill you but were majestic too. It was only made more so as we turned back onto the street, retracing our steps past the can with, "Poetry for Your Soul" written on it. Without stopping, Jordan grabbed the tin and made a sudden turn into the busy street.

"What the-?" I cursed and headed after him.

Car horns rose above the echoing thunder of a hundred engines as drivers swerved in attempts to avoid hitting us. Jordan walked without checking to see if I was following. He seemed to just assume I was right behind him. When he hit the sidewalk on the other side of the road, he continued down Elmwood. Although Jordan was walking, I had to run to keep up with him. His forehead was crinkled with concentration and a sense of urgency flickered in his amber eyes. I couldn't help but wonder how attached Jordan was to the demons he hunted. By hunting demons, he saved humans, but I couldn't help but think maybe he was saving the demons too. Belial had wanted, on some level, to die. There was relief on his face when he went, and I was beginning to think maybe the release was the most important thing to Jordan. He wasn't killing the demons to save the humans, but to save the demons from themselves. It seemed off somehow; however, it didn't feel wrong. I could feel I was right. I couldn't fathom the reasons behind it.

We stopped in front of a large church. It spanned a large section of street with nine doors on the front alone. Fancy windows and detailed stone work made it seem more like a brag show than a place of worship. It was overdone, like a lot of cathedrals, but the aura was different than the buildings around it. It almost glowed like it was alive. The aura shined, pulsating and brilliant, around the entirety of the stone and leaked out into the rest of the city. It was immense, and I couldn't understand how anything could be as enormous as it was.

Jordan took the steps two at a time and headed for the door furthest to the left. He swung it open and stopped, looking in on the service being held. I glanced around him; it was a Christening. The souls of everyone inside the mass were shining at their brightest. The amount of light their hope and faith in their child's future produced was almost blinding. As quietly as possible, Jordan moved toward the collection box. With a bit of magic, he opened the container to put the entire tin can inside.

While he was doing this, I watched the priest bless the baby, and a star seemed to come alive above them. I focused my eyes and saw a being beyond human comprehension. It was constantly shifting and moving, guarded by a light brighter than the sun. Wings spread forth and enveloped the priest, the parents, the godparents, and the infant. The creature's wings made Belial's ones look decrepit in comparison. There was no void I could see around it or above or below it. I was certain beyond all doubt it was an angel. Jordan grabbed me by the shoulder and turned me, so I was no longer looking upon the being. I wanted to see it. I felt as though I needed to see the angel.

When I tried to turn, Jordan held me tight. "Don't you dare turn around."

"Is it an angel? It's so much brighter than Belial was. Are they always so beautiful? Please, I want to see it." I tried to glance over my shoulder, but he grabbed my chin with his hand in order to stop me.

"You have no idea what you're dealing with, Jon. Angels aren't something you screw around with; they are warriors. And, frankly, we can't exactly prove they're good," Jordan admitted and dragged me out into the church's lobby.

I struggled, but Jordan was stronger than me despite the height difference. "How can an angel be bad? Come on, just let me look at it!"

Opening the door, Jordan chucked me outside and closed it gently behind him so as to not interrupt the service. As he did, I ran up the steps to go in another doorway, but Jordan threw me back down and blocked my way. "Putting aside they can turn into demons, this is why they're dangerous. You get enthralled, and you stop doing everything else but thinking about angels. You forget to eat, forget to sleep. Humans can fight against demons; we were made to be able to win over them. Angels... they're another story entirely. We can't fight them; we aren't even a threat to them in the least."

"Please!" I screamed and begged. "Just let me go back! Come on, Jordan! There was an angel in there! Just let me go, please! Please!"

I was on the verge of tears as I struggled kicking and clawing at him in an attempt to escape. He held fast and let me. "You need to calm down or this thing is going to consume you."

"I just... I just." It felt as if my breath was leaving my body and flying back through the church toward the angel. "Please? Please..."

"This is for your own good."

There was frustration coloring his voice as if he was speaking from firsthand experience. I wanted to argue, I did, but the further away he brought me the more I realized he was right. The magnificence remained a picture in my mind, but a clear danger was present when removed from the creature's presence. I took several deep breathes and slowly calmed down enough my thoughts were once again my own.

"Angels?" I felt the single word summed up the unbelievable number of questions.

Jordan shook his head. "Go back to your dorm, Jon."

He waited until I was well on my way before turning and vanishing with a single step. A part of me wanted to turn around and go back to the church, but a voice—like my mother's—snuck up in the back of my mind, stopping me. Ducking my head, I crossed the street into the cemetery and headed back to the dormitories.

Six

If I had expected Jordan to put aside his work to train me, I would have been beyond wrong. Even knowing that, I still kept coming early. Time in the shop meant time with magic, and the more I knew about magic, the closer I was to the nebulous unknown of my father. The shop was empty. Jordan stood behind the counter reading a pile of notebooks. His eyes were bloodshot, and the normally neatly combed locks of his bleached hair were a twisted, tangled mess. I waited for him to say hello. When he didn't greet me or give me some work to do, I sidled closer.

"Norse runes, demons drawn from all types of mythology..." I rambled. He didn't even bother looking up from his notes. "Daughters of Tinashe? Tinashe is from somewhere in South Africa, but Sons of Snorri makes them from Iceland or something."

"They're named after their starting members," he replied.

"Who were?" I asked. When Jordan failed to answer, I slammed my hands down on the counter. "I promised my mother I wasn't going to die. If I want to not die, I need you to work with me. I don't do well without info."

Amber eyes rolled up towards me in a black stare. Despite his lack of height, he seemed gigantic when he straightened. I pulled my hands back from the counter and hoped he wouldn't kick me out. Instead, he told me, "Tinashe was born some thousand years ago. She and her two younger sisters were the first trio to hunt, and they organized their daughters to do the same.

From there, the group grew into the power it is today. They have around five hundred members who are mainly non-magical."

"Why? If my father was a wizard like you, why am I a warlock?" I pressed. If magic came from Hell, it made no sense for it to be some recessive trait.

"The Covenant ensures magic is diluted when it comes in contact with non-magic blood. A wizard and a mortal make a warlock. A warlock and a mortal make a psychic. A psychic and a mortal make a mortal." He tapped his pen against the wooden counter. "It's like a stain, Jon. Bit by bit, the blood not sworn to Hell washes it clean."

"Gross."

Scoffing, Jordan shut his book. "No. Gross is the incest that resulted when some found that out. It wasn't always that way. The Covenant wasn't widely accepted by a majority of magic users until a little over two thousand years ago. Before that, magic had a bit more sway, and the Covenant didn't affect those not sworn to it."

"Cause that makes sense."

"Truth seldom does," he retorted. "It's not like we're working within the realms of logic you grew up with."

"Yeah, like Belial picking up his void!" I pointed out, miming the demon's act. "I get it's made of darkened souls or whatever. I get that, honestly, but all the others hid it like the Dorota or Baoht. What are voids? Stop trying to simplify things for me. I need to learn this stuff."

Jordan cringed. "It's complicated."

"Don't brush me off. I'm so sick of getting brushed aside. I know I'm just a warlock, but if I'm to believe you, that's a lot more than most people get," I said.

Rubbing his eyes, he leaned from the counter. "What part don't you get?"

Part of me wanted to say everything. I didn't get why runes were from Old Norse. Void interactions made no sense at all. Hell was both a place and a state of being. Magic had never been complicated. It had been the easier bit of me. There was no clear starting point, and I suspected Jordan knew as much.

"You grew up with this." He frowned but didn't argue. "What is a void?"

"It really is just an amalgamation of darkened souls, Jon. Most demons don't interact with it because they have survival instincts. There's nothing on Earth like them. I can give you metaphors, but that's it," he explained. When I nodded for him to continue, he shrugged. "It's like a chain made out of souls. The more souls there are, the longer the chain. Warmth and light shortens the chain. When the chain gets too short, they either have to go back to Hell or put their own essence on the line. When Belial transformed, it was his essence which became visible. His last shot of strength before I killed him."

His voice broke on the last bit. Jordan paled, and with a shake of his head, he pushed away from the counter, vanishing into the back hall without a word. I wasn't about to let him get away. Running behind the counter, I followed him into the hall. Fleeing out a side door into the alley, I followed, remaining in the doorway. He stood almost perfectly still save for his hands. They twitched as if to clench into fists, but they stopped each time, and he stretched his fingers back.

"Jordan?" I called cautiously. He didn't respond. Stepping out into the alley, I trudged up beside him. "Jordan?" I asked again, reaching out to put a hand on his shoulder.

He jumped and backed away. "Go back inside, Jon."

"You can't keep brushing me off." There was only so many times a guy could stand being ignored.

He licked his lips. Rocking back and forth, he went from still to an explosion of fidgeting movement. His hands clenched fully and unclenched. Tossing a hand to the side, he sent tendrils of fire down one end of the alley while his other hand shot lightning at the ground. Jordan gritted his teeth, and I jumped back. The stoic calm I'd come to expect from Jordan had shattered. While his expressions had aged him before, he looked almost younger than me in his strange tantrum.

"I killed him," he snarled. "I killed the one creature on this forsaken rock who had done anything for me." He slammed his fist into the other side of the alley. I hoped nobody was home to feel the foundation shake beneath the strength of Jordan's strike. "I didn't grow up in this, boy. I grew up with a suicidal maniac for a mother and a father who'd rather have set the entire world on fire than help a single living soul! His own son included! You want to know why there're so few magic users left? Do you?" Jordan stormed at me. He got right up in my face with all five foot nine of his height and towered like Goliath. "You can thank Ezekiel Ostairius. He left over five hundred screaming in pain in a single night."

The ground beneath my feet shook. Waves of magic radiated off Jordan like heat off a sun struck summer black top. Tears gathered at the corners of his eyes, but they just burned away before falling. The only other person I'd ever seen so upset had been my mother after I'd told her about seeing demons. She'd been so strong. After answering all my questions, she'd assured me that I was safe and sent me to bed. When I couldn't sleep, I had snuck back downstairs where she'd been curled up on the couch caught between crying and whispering hateful things towards the window. The way she'd talked had been like she'd been talking to my father. I didn't know how to deal with her then, and I was no better off now.

"I... I'm sorry?" Condolences and reassurances weren't my strong suit.

All at once, the power was gone. Jordan let out a huffed laugh then wiped his hands across his face. "Forget it, Jon. Thankfully, you have a good and decent mother, and your father wasn't around to screw you up." I went to defend my dad, but he silenced me with a glare. "Magic is waning. One day, it will be gone. All demons will creep back to Hell having no way to refill their voids. The world would be better without us." After a moment, he added in a whisper, "And that was the only thing my father ever got right."

"You want to talk about it?" I asked though I wasn't sure talking would be helpful.

He patted me on the shoulder before walking by me back into the shop. Following, I tried not to be disappointed. The first break in Jordan's mask, and he'd put it back on like his breakdown was nothing. Pausing in the hall, I slipped out my cell. Making sure Jordan was out of sight, I quickly typed out a message to my mom in hopes that she'd know what to do. She simply typed back: *Respect his privacy.* I shoved the phone back into my pocket and trudged back into the store. Jordan had collected his notebooks. He shoved them into a small black backpack.

"We're done."

"What?" My heart sank. "I didn't do anything wrong. I mean, if I pushed you too much or... I can do better," I promised though I had no idea what I'd done wrong. "I know I'm slow, and it's weird 'cause normally I'm a fast learner, but this is so new and important. I swear I take this super seriously. I swear I can be better."

Jordan zipped up the bag. "For today, Jon. We're done for today."

Air flooded back into my lungs. My nerves ached, having been torn to shreds in a single second. I nodded, not trusting myself to speak. His eyes flickered over my face, but they never met mine. Jordan turned his back to me. Swinging on his backpack, he stretched his fingers straight again before squeezing them into fists.

"I'm sorry." The words slipped out despite my best attempts to press my teeth together.

"I just need to be around friends." I had thought we were friends. "Somewhere I can vent some of this." He gestured vaguely at himself. "I've got an open invitation to George's, and I haven't seen his youngest yet, and she's almost two."

My head heated up like a strange fever. Blood rushed in my ears. Nodding again, I clenched my jaw so hard I was sure my teeth would crack. I was his apprentice. I'd offered to listen. We were closer in age than he and George were. What made George so great? George was a psychic. I was a warlock. My father had been Jordan's childhood friend. If anybody's kid was important, I should have been. Ignoring every petty thought racing through my head, I kept nodding until the shop was dark, and we both stood outside on the street.

He mounted his bike and commanded, "Go back to your dorm." Right before he sped out of sight, he mumbled, "I need to be around someone who doesn't make me feel so guilty."

Rooted to the cement, I wanted to implode and explode at the same time. I had done nothing, and he had no right to put his guilt on me. I hadn't made him kill Belial. I hadn't been the one who challenged the demon, and I certainly wasn't the one who decided to go down that street knowing Belial haunted the curb there. None of this was my fault. Still, my stomach tied itself in knots. My hands felt too big as did my feet. I was a walking, talking mess of a clown who had screwed up somewhere without even knowing it. Shoving my oversized hands into my sweatshirt pocket, I ducked my head down and stooped my shoulders as I headed back to my dorm.

Seven

"A rave?" I grimaced. "I don't think a rave is a good idea."

Slamming the pile of books on the counter, Jordan glowered. "A good idea? No, it's the only choice. Maxwell 'Cheshire' Ericson doesn't show up elsewhere on a regular basis. He doesn't have an address and he doesn't stick in a town long. If they're going to get him to stay, our best chance of knowing is by going because they'll have to approach him during it. He doesn't keep a cell phone; he doesn't use electronics outside of his music. Even the sound is manipulated airwaves done magically because he's not the type to be solidly in the everyday, normal happy human world you so moronically believe we all live in. Some of us have more important things to do!"

"Point taken, but why a rave?"

"Because he likes raves, I don't have a rationale for everything. Cheshire Max does raves in the closest city following a hunt. He cleared out an infestation in Victor at someone's request." Jordan gestured at the note George had left in the morning.

I picked up the note. It just said the guy's name. "Seriously? How do you know George is right?"

"He's a psychic. He doesn't hunt. He does recon." He waved the paper. "This is what he does with his magic. It's dangerous, but he contributes more than most psychics. And on top of everything else, he's got a nine to five heading some company's financial division from home with his two kids!"

Jordan vanished through the wall, and I blinked. When he didn't immediately reappear, I leaned over the counter. Nope, he hadn't ducked down there. I moved a bit to the left and squinted. Magic or not—I couldn't see a doorway there. Glancing around, I determined no one else was in the store and jumped over the counter. Walking forward, I nearly jumped out of my skin when Jordan walked back through the wall and looked over at me like I was the fly in his soup.

"What the—?" I flailed gesturing at the wall.

Jordan shrugged. "Door."

Turning back to the wall, I took a step forward and walked into a solid wall because Jordan was a vindictive man. I swore and rubbed my head. "Not a door!"

"You are seriously the thickest person I've ever met," Jordan said pulling me a few inches to the right and shoving me forward again.

I gave a manly shout of surprise and covered my head with my arms. When I didn't immediately hit wall, I opened one eye. To my left was a bunch of shelving units with books. I shuffled and looked to the right, and there was a door marked as an employee bathroom. Letting my hands drop to my sides, I turned in a circle to see Jordan facing me and leaning back against the counter with his arms folded over his chest.

"So—door?" I drew a little door in the air, and he nodded. "Magic?"

"Architectural illusion like the Labyrinth," Jordan replied turning back to his organizational work.

Knowing I would be ignored, I wandered down to glance at the books. It had been three days since my last adventure, which left me on my lucky Wednesday afternoon off. While my friends protested morning classes, I was pretty content with an eight in the morning lecture on marketing trends in social media. It left me free, and right now an open schedule was a good schedule, though I knew a few of my friends had begun to suspect I had met a local girl at some party. Eventually, they would get curious and find out about the shop and Jordan. I could only hope that their one-track minds didn't think something so far off base, but maybe the more romantic direction would be less suspicious. I couldn't go about explaining magic to them.

"Don't touch anything," Jordan grumbled marching past me to grab another box of what looked like handmade journals. "And don't speak Latin to the books."

"Latin? Seriously? Do these books do spells? Will they get excited?" I immediately grabbed one off the shelf. "Incendio!"

Jordan snatched the book from my hand. "Fantasy boarding school Latin?" His eyes narrowed, and his face got this pinched look. He smacked me on the side of the head with the book and slammed it back into place on the shelf. "These are modern texts. Excited books—dear goodness."

He turned around and went back out into the main area of the store. Rubbing the area where he'd hit, I followed, more than slightly disappointed the books wouldn't set stuff on fire accidentally. Jordan opened the tiny, little door separating the counter from the rest, and I walked through it and sat down in the chair facing the counter up by the bay window.

"It won't be until late tonight. A text which..." He pulled out a phone. "This phone will receive and provide the location. You need to be prepared to go at eleven tonight."

"Eleven?" I frowned. "I have class tomorrow."

"Then do class and go away now. I've no use for you today besides the rave," Jordan said. He cut the sides of the box he had just emptied and tossed it back into the hidden hallway.

I pulled out my phone and scrolled through my schedule. Tomorrow—Thursday, no tests or anything, and technically, class didn't start until ten. I could just grab jeans and shower and stuff afterwards, but what about breakfast? I loved breakfast. I did have those bars, or I could just grab a bagel on my way to class. It would be sort of out of my way; maybe Greg would grab me something from the dining hall. I could always play sick.

"Eleven?" I asked, knowing I was getting myself into trouble.

Jordan glanced up with a smirk. "Eleven—dress for a rave."

"Yeah." I walked out of the shop to do my best to prep for tonight and tomorrow's rush to class. "How do I dress for a rave?"

The rest of the day was spent between searching images online of rave clothes, feeling terribly out of place knowing I would end up at one, and studying. My homework was done, so the guilt I was feeling shouldn't have been there, but I actually liked my classes which made it more difficult. The transition from afternoon to evening kind of went by unnoticed after I got distracted looking up some new trailers and spoilers for upcoming comic superhero films. I would say I wasn't proud, but a certain captain told me to never apologize for being a geek. Ultimately, when ten-thirty rolled around, I went into a raging mess ending with Tyson—my loving roommate—tossing his pillow at my head and telling me to get my dumb butt—censored for your pleasure—out of the room. I walked down the stairs feeling extremely awkward when my phone beeped with a text: *Here*. The number was unknown, but I had a pretty good idea who it was considering the time. Walking out of the dorm with a confused glance from the gamers who had taken over the lobby, I glanced around and saw Jordan glowering down at the cell George had given him.

He glanced up from his phone and stared for a moment before chuckling. He gestured at my jeans and button-up black dress shirt then bent over laughing so hard there wasn't a sound. The reaction destroyed his nicely cultivated cool persona with fitted dark-wash jeans, a black belt and matching boots, a white shirt and black leather jacket. His hair was spiked, and his eyebrows were black making his white hair look even stranger. The only oddity I noticed besides him nearly suffocating from laughter was his black painted nails.

"What?" I asked opening my arms to gesture at my outfit. "I don't have club clothes."

"A dress shirt? Good thing you aren't going out aiming to get laid." Jordan snickered. "We're meeting Cheshire Max at his rave. Let's get moving."

"Nice nail polish," I grumbled trying to regain some ground, but he merely smirked.

"Going for the late 90s vampire look." He tossed me the other helmet to his bike.

I caught it and sighed. "Where to?"

Jordan sat on his bike and waited for me to get settled before replying, "Old metal working facility out near Henrietta."

We sped away before I had time to question anything. I knew raves were sometimes pulled together at random locations, or so the internet had told me, but it didn't mean I was any more comfortable with a rusty old factory. The drive wasn't terribly long, but the whole trip took enough time for me to wonder how I had ended up going to my first rave with my magic teacher. He wasn't too much older than me—couldn't be more than twenty-five tops, but he was so much more at ease in his body. I could only hope it came with time. Unfortunately, I was getting the idea it came with growing up hunting demons. Either way, he rested in a world conceived apart from the concrete realities I embraced from my mother.

Jordan parked the bike on the side of a huge warehouse. The security lights were off, and I could hear the bass line from outside though I couldn't see the lights. Placing my helmet alongside his, I glanced around nervously. The parking lot was empty, and I had the feeling we weren't exactly supposed to be there.

"Stay close," Jordan ordered before opening the door and unleashing the blinding strobe lights.

The pulsing mass released an acrid perfume with each slamming wave of their bodies against one another's. Lights swirled without cords or electronics. The fact nobody noticed the magic at work all around them baffled me. The DJ danced and spun his records turning one song into five into one again moving between techno, punk, rock, and random movie phrases. Though the smell was sort of off-putting, the experience was something I appreciated. Now, I wasn't entirely sure where to go from the metal deck which wound around the room. The DJ was set up on the side opposite from the door on a platform on top of the deck while the dancers were in a pit down a small flight of stairs. Metal decks wove up and around the room on multiple levels with some people dancing on the stairs and upper levels. Others were passing out drinks and glowing accessories from bits which went in your mouth to the necklace, ring, and bracelet staples to far stranger whips some people attached to their belts and gauges.

Cheshire Max didn't exactly look like the sort of guy I pictured a demon hunter would be. He didn't have an addiction to flannel. There weren't any grizzly scars. Jordan hadn't any either. Cheshire Max had long, coiling dreadlocks tied up and tangled into a knot on the back of his head. The buff guy swung one arm in the air jumping around in a black sleeveless shirt and cargo shorts. Jordan took a step toward the DJ deck but stopped as two women slipped by us and moved toward Cheshire Max.

"Seriously?" he grumbled and dragged me down onto the dance floor.

I didn't have dance skills. Jordan sort of pulsed along with the crowd melding with them and easing his way directly toward Cheshire while I awkwardly followed to the glares of those who I accidentally interrupted. I held up my hands trying to apologize over the ever increasing volume, but the dancers went back to their games rather quickly. They weren't looking for a fight.

Though his body followed the flow of the mass, Jordan's eyes glanced between me and the pair of girls winding up the stairs to Cheshire Max. They didn't seem so extraordinary. Both had dark hair and eyes with tanned skin. They were kind of on the thin side but definitely fit, like runners. They were also undoubtedly related, with the elder covered in intricate tattoos. The gears clicked in my head when the elder glanced over her shoulder, and I wanted to hit myself for being so slow. They were Madrid and Rio. Jordan grabbed my arm and pulled me along with him down beneath the metal platform. Breathing in, he exhaled, and the sound melted away to a bearable background hum.

"How?" I asked only to have Jordan hold up a hand causing me to drop the question.

From beneath, I could see Max's bare feet and the gold-brown of his dreads through the grates. His face was covered in stubble, and his brows were like rectangles over his eyes. His face was narrow with a pointed nose and continuous smile. He beamed and threw his hands up when Rio sauntered toward him

with a sway in her hip going down her leather pants and bright
red high heels. Rio's tattoos were insane. Both arms were sleeved
in animals and symbols vibrating with the amount of innate
magic. Madrid was dressed the same with the same backless,
loose gold scaled top.

"Cheshire." Rio's voice was like honey with this pull around
the vowels. It was sugary sweet, and she opened her arms,
hugging him. "It's so good to see you."

I mouthed, "Spanish?" to Jordan who glared and held up a
hand to silence me before he rolled his eyes and replied, "Peruvian."

Meanwhile, Cheshire Max spun Rio around, dancing with
her while the music thundered on. His accent was similarly
foreign, but in an entirely different direction—probably British—
as he said, "Rio! I haven't seen you in years! Where have you
been?"

"Oh, you know," she said pulling away and bringing Madrid
closer to her.

Pulling one dreadlock, the rest tumbled down swaying with
his continuous movements. "Madrid? You're all grown up!" He
didn't hug her though he seemed to want to. She had a much
more standoffish pose than her aunt. Madrid's arms were crossed
over her chest and she radiated impatience.

"She's a bit stubborn about learning other languages." Rio
shrugged apologetically.

Frowning, Max glanced at Madrid. "Pity 'bout that. I can
spell her with tongues if she'd like."

Rio turned to her niece. *"¿Quieres que él hechice que tu puedes
hablar en lenguas desconocidas?"*

Cheshire's great eyebrows knotted waiting for an answer.
Madrid nodded, and I wanted to swear as the air in the room
shifted, and Max proclaimed, "I should do it at every party!
Think of it—why hello there—goodness, you speak French
fluently! What? You're speaking Yiddish! It'd be brilliant."

A tight smile pushed back Madrid's face in a tense expression. "I certainly appreciate it." The words vibrated like there
were multiple layers to the sounds.

"I'm so glad you got the message. I'm never sure how it'll work out considering." He didn't explain what exactly should be considered, but both Madrid and Rio nodded.

"I was pleased to hear you'd be in town. I have a new friend who I think you'd be interested in meeting." Rio pressed a hand against Cheshire Max's chest, and his smile fell away as his eyes flicked down to her hand and then to Madrid.

"I know who your friend is Rio, and sorry, but I have no interest in him or his ideas."

Jordan frowned when Max replied, which didn't make sense to me. I hadn't thought we wanted anyone joining in on the summoning. George had been nervous about what Mammon could do if brought about, which didn't make sense to me. If demons could naturally wander onto Earth through voids, there was no reason a summoning would do anything to help the son of the Devil. I could only assume there was something George and Jordan knew which I didn't.

Rio's smile didn't fall away though she let her hand slide back to her side before coming to rest on her hip when he stepped away from her. "We need a fifth, Cheshire."

"No."

Madrid frowned. "We will be summoning the first-born. Great risks yield great rewards."

Cheshire Max shook his head, letting his dreads swing. "Or great falls."

He turned back to his music when Madrid stretched forward grabbing hold of his wrist. Cheshire Max spun, throwing his other hand forward with his palm facing Madrid. She flew back into the railing of the metal deck over twenty feet away. Rio's eyes narrowed moving between Madrid and Cheshire, analyzing the situation carefully. The tiger on her left arm stirred and paced down her arm through the ruins to her wrist. Its tail flicked before it yawned, stretching its jaws. Rio rested her right hand against the tiger sending it back up her arm to return to its original position.

"Where do you stand?" she asked, placing her hands on her hips. "Against, with, or neutral."

"You know me, Rio; always neutral," Cheshire Max replied turning back to his music. "Your soul is your own to destroy."

"We will use him against his own kind. We could save hundreds." She held up a hand when Madrid moved to approach. Fire flickered across the younger woman's skin.

"Use him? Mammon?" The name resonated throughout the hall, and the music stuttered, causing the dancers to falter for a moment and something flickered at the edge of the room. "Isn't a weapon to be used? Mammon..." The room shuddered again, and I turned toward the door as the hairs on the back of my neck stood on end. "Will kill mortal after mortal for the glory of Hell. Mammon..." The door opened. Black smoke billowed in though the music had returned, leaving the dancers back in their mass trance. "Will use you."

"Jordan?" I whispered, and he held up a hand, but the gesture wasn't good enough this time. "Jordan, we've got a problem."

Jordan grabbed me turning my gaze upwards once more. Rio was backing away never breaking eye contact with Cheshire Max. Madrid rushed to her side, and they ran without another word. Cheshire Max crouched down low to the ground and tapped the metal with a smirk. His blue eyes staring straight into my own as runes lit across the deck and the entire room flooded with figure eights and runes. The darkness at the door faded, and a passerby closed the door without a second thought.

"Jordan—what was that?" I asked, no longer whispering, when Cheshire Max jumped up, jogging down the stairs.

"How many times has the name been said today?" Jordan replied.

"Only three." I counted.

Jordan smiled. "And yesterday, how many times?"

"A dozen or so, I guess. I don't know. Prudence said it like, three times at least," I said, not sure exactly what he was getting at, but I guessed anyways. "Names have power, right? He's one of five who understands the use of names—right?"

"Correct. Now think, you're aware of your name all around the world—but so many people say it without knowing—mortals, so you start to narrow your range to only pick up on the patterns.

Your name starts picking up in a city..." He dragged out the end of the word when Cheshire Max popped into the bubble with a grin.

"Jordan!" He was taller than I had thought. He stood a good two inches above me. The dude was a giant, and he waved his arms as if to hug Jordan before pulling back just to shake hands. "Good to see you! Never thought you'd be involved in a rogue hunt. Tell George thanks for the note." He turned to me. "How are you? Can I get you a drink?"

"I'm good."

He didn't believe me. "Are you sure? George said you were new at this."

"We haven't been here too long," I assured him.

Cheshire's eyes were so bright blue they looked like they were lit by a black light. "Do you remember the last time we partied together?"

He started to dance again, bouncing back and forth, twirling his dreads, a completely relaxed smile on his face. Jordan ran a hand through his hair then gestured at the crowd. "Don't you have a show to run?"

"Hmm—I can do it from down here—or even better, let's get pancakes! The American kind!" His hands reached up, grabbing hold of the grates, swinging up and turning himself upside down. "Oh, the one with the large stacks and red velvet kind!"

Jordan glanced at me, and I said, "I think there's one in Irondequoit."

"Do you need to get back to the dorm? You have—something—right?" He gestured vaguely then headed up the stairs of the deck with a dancing Cheshire Max bouncing after us with a lot of jumps. He climbed up everything we came across. I wasn't about to miss this awkward diner experience.

"I couldn't sleep yet if I wanted to—food sounds good." At eighteen, I could eat at any time of day anyways. I searched through my pants for my wallet, but Jordan shoved my wallet back toward my pocket when I finally pulled it out.

"My treat," he said, and relief washed over me. Pancakes were great, but free pancakes were even better.

"You know, you remind me of somebody." Cheshire Max drew closer up to me before he flicked the door open and let it shut behind him. The music never stopped even as we left. The pulsing bass still hummed even after the door closed.

"Ah—my dad was a hunter," I offered, uncertain where he was going.

"Dad—no—you're too young," he retorted before leaning in close. "It was a long time ago—he was." Max turned to Jordan. "That bloke—oh..." He frowned. "Penny board." He jumped subjects completely, pulling out a mini skate board. "Like the old days."

Jordan shrugged like this was usual but then stopped and reached out, preventing me from going toward the bike. "The utter douche."

The bike was melted down. The tires were flat and cut all to pieces. The metal was melted on the pavement, and the helmets were smashed to pieces on the ground. A line beneath one of the lights caught my eye, and I turned back to the building. Underneath one of the security lights, spelled out in liquid metal—still steaming though it was likely solid again already—was one word: *Mine.*

"Oh." Cheshire Max stepped back, turning around cautiously. "Not a good sign."

"He's not here," Jordan reassured. "The utter douche." He swore again poking at his destroyed bike with his foot.

"You have another, right? I could get you a board," Cheshire Max offered, holding out his own. "Less shadows."

"Yeah, but it takes more magic to get around quickly on. I have my older one somewhere back at the shop." He shook his head, turning to face the taller magic user. "League walk?"

"I guess, but I always get fuzzy in cities. We could warp fold directly there if the kid's been there before," Max suggested gesturing at me with his penny board.

"Never been there," I admitted. "And—league walking? Warp fold? Are we in a fairy tale or outer space?"

Jordan faked a dry laugh, glaring at me. "You aren't trained enough to warp fold even if you had been there before. He's only a warlock," he noted to Max. "I can warp fold us there. Just don't get sick on my shoes."

Warp folding wasn't like jumping through space NASA fantasy style. Jordan pulled apart a small hole and a sign came into view as he expanded the hole wider and wider until the entire pancake house came into view and the hole was the size of a door. Max moved to stand pressed up at Jordan's side, and Jordan grabbed me, bringing me similarly close on his opposite side before stepping forward and pulling on the image. The air around us popped like we had been in a bubble. There we were—in the parking lot of the pancake house, which was luckily open 24/7. Cheshire Max cheered and walked up from the asphalt to the door, going through, while Jordan turned and pulled at something causing the hole behind us to collapse. Stepping forward away from Jordan, I promptly hurled. Fortunately, I missed his feet and my own. Unfortunately, some poor guy's tires got the brunt as I leaned against the car trying to catch my breath as another wave of nausea came over me.

Jordan slapped me on the back. "Not the most enjoyable transport. Let's get inside."

"My mouth tastes so bad," I mumbled as Jordan guided me around the barf.

"I'll buy you a coffee too," he offered and immediately requested waters and coffees—decaf for me—for all of us. Squishing into the seat opposite from Cheshire Max, Jordan sat down in the booth beside me. The lights were bright above us and my eyes hurt almost as much as the rest of me.

"I hate warp folding," I grumbled letting my head fall on the table.

Max thanked the waiter who handed him his extra-large coffee. "Why? It's no worse than a hangover."

"I've never been drunk—like, hangover drunk," I admitted into the table.

"Oh—you're not legal yet. Right, America."

Jordan nudged me, pushing my small decaf coffee at me. I took the warm brew in both hands and drank slowly. The liquid wasn't the best coffee I've ever had, but considering how nicely it replaced the vile taste in my mouth, the drink was the most gorgeous piece of the night. The laminated menu was laid upon the table beside me by Jordan while Cheshire Max grinned, flipping through the few pages of pancake options.

"This is my favorite part." Max beamed before gulping another hot mouthful of coffee. "All these different choices. Visiting you is the best."

"I'm just glad you said no," Jordan said glancing through the healthier options on the menu before giving up and placing it on the table. "These binges are terrible for you. Consistent eating is the healthier option. If you ate daily like mortals, you wouldn't be starved after every hunt."

Despite Jordan's scolding words, Max continued to smile widely. "I just forget. There's too much to do." He then became distracted with the menu. "Where'd the red velvet go?"

When the waitress—an older woman with graying hair and tired brown eyes—came around, I scrambled to look at the menu while Jordan said, "Breakfast sampler—no pancakes and a glass of orange juice."

"I would like the bananas and cream Belgian waffles with the strawberry banana cream pie pancakes, and another coffee." Max paused flipping the menu back and forth. "A side of chips too."

"Chips? We don't have chips," the waitress replied. Her name tag read Jennie.

"Fries," Jordan translated.

"Fries, okay—no problem." She didn't exactly smile but gave him this exhausted look of gratitude.

I flipped back through before just giving up and ordering. "The quick two-egg I guess... with some tea?"

"We have black and citrus as well as a lovely iced tea," Jennie informed me.

"Is the black caffeinated?" When she nodded, I glanced back at the menu. "Then citrus."

She took the laminated menus and vanished back toward the kitchen. Max went about fiddling with straw wrappers and sugar packets while Jordan idly carved runes into the bottom of the table with a paperclip. I, however, couldn't help but stare at the tiny desserts card they stick at every table. Pulling out my phone, I grimaced at the time. Even though it was only ten past one, it was still morning now instead of night.

"Nine hours—how many hours? It would be like seven hours to sleep? Six?" I shifted in my seat and searched out the waitress hoping our food had been prepared already. However, there was no sign of waitress Jennie or anything close to resembling our food even though we were the only patrons currently in the joint.

"Six hours? You should have yourself a lie in," Max suggested. "Eight hours at least every night—more around ten for a good relaxing lie in."

"Classes," I replied.

"Missing one class isn't going to kill your grade," Jordan informed me. I made a noncommittal noise in response.

When Jennie returned to the table like a glorious, food-bearing goddess, my heart swelled. I took the hot plate and gorged myself alongside Max. Jordan ate methodically. I could feel his eyes bouncing from me to Max.

"What?" I grumbled, leaning over my food protectively.

Jordan raised an eyebrow. "Just making sure you're breathing."

Max's head snapped up from his waffles; his dreads jumped with the momentum. "Someone's listening," he whispered. His eyes grew wide as he stared straight ahead between Jordan and me.

Jordan slowly put down his fork. He glanced over his shoulder toward the window Max was watching. I swiveled in my seat. On the opposite side of the glass, an older man stood in a black suit with a white dress shirt. His hands rested on a black cane, and his fingers were covered in rings. Piercing blue eyes burned right through us on a tanned face. Dark gray hair was tethered at the nape of his neck. The bulb of his nose sat a bit lower on his face, and with his thin lips, I was thinking an Italian Hannibal the Cannibal. Hopefully the look was the only commonality. Wrinkled and weathered tan skin hung heavy about his brow. The weight of his stare pulled his dark eyebrows low. The two lines of hair rounded at the outer corners drew his face downwards beneath the tension in the wrinkles above them.

When I first turned, the man had not been smiling. His lips were pulled taut, but seeing us all looking his way, the corners of his mouth ascended. The expression wasn't pleasant. Caught somewhere between forced and practiced. He was probably no taller than Jordan and bowed his head in greeting one at a time to Max, me, and, with a narrowing of his eyes, Jordan.

"Who's that?" I asked turning back around.

Jordan and Max continued to stare unblinkingly at the man. After a long moment, Jordan said, "Giuseppe."

Looking back over the booth, I saw the odd smile grow colder. The lights in the restaurant flickered before dimming, and behind Giuseppe, a veritable army of demons came into view. They weren't a species I had seen before. They stood on four legs with their heads about the same height as Giuseppe's shoulders. Spiraling horns curled from their heads like mountain goats. Each tip dripping thick red. The seconds ticked, and one at a time the beasts tossed their heads, splattering the glass with blood. Skeletal faces patched with muscles stretched out. They flexed their jaws as if they were adjusting to the constraint. Baring their teeth, even from a distance, the lack of tongues was glaringly obvious. Large spikes stuck up behind their heads upon their shoulders while their tails were docked, or at least I assumed considering they were only a couple of bones tied together with connective tissue.

"I'm not exactly in the mood for a stand-off." Max sighed, finally moving his attention to me. "If things start going south, I'd suggest you be the one to get the mortals out."

I looked to Jordan who shook his head without changing his focus. "He's posturing. Giuseppe has always valued magic too much to attack an apprentice and a neutral party. He'll wait until I'm alone."

"I can't leave you alone against a pack." Max leaned forward against the table pushing the remains of his meal aside.

"You remember where the store is?"

Max frowned. "I said I'm not leaving you to deal with him alone. We can wait him out."

Jordan slid from the booth and tossed a hundred dollar bill

down on the table. His eyes remained trained on Giuseppe. "You are going to take the kid to the store. Jon—" He glanced at me out of the corner of his eye. "The amulet you had—your dad's?"

"I got it on," I told him, and his eyes refocused outside.

Had he been nervous about me? He was the idiot going up against an army of half-dead giant hounds. He was going to die. There was no way he could survive those things. Whatever exhaustion had been dragging at me after the warp was gone. Jitters ran down my legs and arms. Jordan was screwed. More hounds kept joining. If this was posturing, Giuseppe was an overachiever.

"The amulet should protect you on the way home even if he decides to try something." Jordan's brows knotted as if he wasn't certain he was completely content with the option. "Max, you haven't been anywhere on the University of Rochester campus before, right?"

Max frowned. "I can get him as far as the Chinese restaurant on Wilson and Elmwood."

"Get out the back," Jordan said and stormed forwards toward Giuseppe who turned and headed toward the door.

"There's only one door," I protested, but he was already gone.

Max grabbed my arm and nearly hefted me over the table. I raced to keep up with him, but he practically dragged me regardless. Jennie was nowhere to be found, and no one stopped us as Max fled through the kitchen. The cook stood flipping through a red book with dragons on the cover completely oblivious as we rushed past. Max kicked another door open. Fresh air hit me along with the stale smell of trash and smoke. Jennie leaned against the building with a cigarette in her hand. The cigarette was at her lips, and her cheeks were hallowed with her inhale, but she was frozen. The bit of smoke lingered at her lips failing to rise or dissipate.

Before I could even begin to argue or question what in the Seventh night was going on with the whole slow motion bit, Max was tearing the fabric of reality apart and pulling a Chinese food delivery service to us. The low growls of dogs vibrated through the air, but the noise shook, hollow and rolling. Max did warp folding differently. While Jordan's movements had been neat and precise, Max tore quickly and snapping the world into place around us faster. One moment, there was barking, the next, I was stumbling forward experiencing the now increasingly familiar nausea. Max threw me down the street and slammed the hole behind us.

"Are you all right?" He leaned over me then jumped up, spinning in a circle though I hadn't heard a sound. "Can you get back on your own? I'd like to not wait too much longer to warp to the shop if you think you're good."

I pulled myself up and started running. Adrenaline coursed through me, and I almost forgot to yell, "Good."

Feeling a warp without being part was off putting. I didn't watch, but when he went through, the world rippled and caught me mid-step. I tripped, falling in a tight tumble before getting up groggily and running once again. The amulet might protect me, but I wasn't nearly as confident in its abilities against hellhounds. They had to be hellhounds. Those canine monstrosities were either hellhounds or corpses. The horns pushed me toward the whole demonic line of thinking. My lungs burned. My mouth tasted like crap, but my head was leveled. The dorms were a good few minutes away even running. I could see the dull lights in my mind's eye. I needed to be there as soon as possible. The earth hummed. Though colors flickered beneath lights from various buildings, I blinded my mind to the demons. I hoped if I did not look too closely at them, they would not concentrate on me.

I was not so lucky. When I left Wilson to cut from Schlegel between Lattimore and the Strong Auditorium, a humanoid form slinked forth from the Wilson Quadrangle. Sliding to a stop, I collapsed to the ground barely five feet from him. I was certain my life was going to end right there. The man—I couldn't find a void in the end though I didn't know one way or another whether I had just missed it or it was so big I couldn't hope to see the difference—had white hair like Jordan and purple eyes. He smiled at me and held out a hand as if to help me up without closing the distance. I pushed myself to my feet, and his smile fell away. He was about my height and just as lanky. The skinniness of his limbs was accentuated by his dark skinny jeans and long-sleeved shirt. His skin was either unnaturally pale, or the light was playing a trick on my eyes. Or he was a demon. It would explain the kind of light blue tinge to him.

"You okay?" he asked.

I walked in a circle around him, and he stood still turning to keep his eyes focused on me. When I was on the opposite side, I said, "I'm fine."

"You were running like a bat out of..." he trailed off with a smirk. "Well, you know. Sure you're okay?"

The comparison bothered me. The phrase was appropriate, yet the fact the person I had run into had said something regarding the demonic had me freaked. Paranoid or not, I wasn't risking sticking around to find out. I took a few steps backwards and shrugged.

"Just in a rush to get home," I told him and made a run for it.

When I got to the dorm, I glanced back, and he was still standing there with his hands in his pockets watching me. His white hair looked like a halo from the distance. I pulled out my keycard and slammed the door tightly behind me, causing the gamers who had fallen asleep in the lobby area to jump up and glower at me. By the time I had gotten up to my room and shucked my clothes to sink into bed, I had myself convinced I had just run into a normal human guy walking around campus.

Eight

I enjoyed school, and this second semester of university shouldn't have been any different, but here I was at the end of March staring out the window in the middle of my introductory course to economics thinking about how much it sucked that it was snowing. Now, I loved snow as much as the next New England kid, but Rochester had to be the weirdest city on the east coast seasons-wise. One day it was spring and the next winter. I hadn't heard from Jordan since the night before, and my brain was firing blanks after a rough night with little sleep. The second the clock ticked to four, I flew out the door; however, Tyson and Mike were close behind catching and flanking me.

"So?" Tyson grinned. "You going to tell me about this party you ran out on at eleven? I heard the motorcycle—was it yours?"

"Mine, no." I shook my head trying desperately to give the impression he was absolutely insane. I pulled out my gloves and put them on as we walked. "It was just a party. Didn't end up staying."

I wasn't sure exactly what to say to get them to leave me alone considering how I'd been blowing them off for Jordan. Plus, Tyson had nearly clobbered me for waking him up before two in the morning. My vomiting in the trash also didn't help.

"Party? Last night? What party? It was a weeknight." Mike looked around me at Tyson. "It's got to be a girl. He'd never go out late for some party."

"Hey, it was a Cheshire Max Rave." I tried to act like the

86

words meant something, and to my surprise, Mike threw an arm out and stopped us in the middle of the hallway.

"Cheshire Max—the Cheshire Max—the DJ?" Mike crowed with delight.

Tyson glanced around nervously. "Who is Cheshire Max?"

"Only the best DJ of this decade! His raves are incredible. There's video online, and messages get sent out like an hour before it starts." He pulled out his phone and opened up a link. "See?" He held it out, showing Cheshire Max spinning his dreadlocks around and playing an insane remix. "This was in Brighton, UK. It's my dream! Man." He smacked my chest. "Why didn't you tell me?"

I shrugged and kept walking. "A friend invited me. I didn't know it was a big deal until we got there, and then we ended up leaving early and going out for pancakes."

"You were high, weren't you?" Tyson accused.

"What? No, course not."

Mike's thumbs flew across the screen and he swore, shoving the phone back in my face. It was Cheshire Max, Jordan, and me in the parking lot from last night. I couldn't help it. I grabbed his phone and swore. Jordan was blurred in the picture like something out of a bad vampire novel while Max was throwing his hands in the air. It was right before we discovered the bike.

"Who took that?" I clicked through to the site, but it was a disconnected link. Glancing down at the URL, I swore again. The address was to a website called *The Fifth*. I couldn't possibly place which one it was, but it had to be one of the rogues.

"You went for pancakes with Cheshire Max himself! You probably didn't even appreciate his sound." Mike threw back his head in exaggerated lamentations.

"I appreciated it," I said because telling him I liked the fact Max was using magic not actual records wasn't an option.

"Yeah right," Mike groused.

Tyson rolled his eyes. "Lay off him, Mike. Jon—where're you headed now?"

"Book shop." I wasn't sure if lying was the best idea, but I knew they'd come with if I didn't, so I went for it. "Got a part-time job."

Tyson gave me a suspicious look, but when Mike opened his mouth, Tyson stopped him. "Mike, let's get to work on the econ project. That way brainiac will have something to work with when he gets back rather than us just begging off him."

"Sure, I'm the brainiac." I snorted though I shouldn't have put too much protest in considering he was helping me.

"Fine, but if you get another invite," Mike grumbled before Tyson pulled him away back toward the dorm.

Shoving my hat on, I headed off through the snow across town toward the bookshop, arriving a bit later than planned, but Jordan was sitting calmly reading a book at the table in the bay window. The little angel rang, and I sighed in relief as warmth returned to my fingers. I slid off my backpack and let it fall to the floor, followed by my gloves and hat. A brilliant, juicy hamburger with fries sat before me on the table. Free food was wonderful.

I sat down and started on my burger as Jordan finished his and moved on to fries. "How many magic users are there currently in the world?"

Jordan raised an eyebrow and chewed thoughtfully for a moment. "Thirteen wizards, twenty-four mages, seventy-two warlocks, eighty-nine magicians, and one hundred and thirty-three psychics. So—about three hundred and thirty-one in all."

"You know the number off the top of your head?" I gawked at him in disbelief. "Seriously, did you just count them?" Jordan shrugged, flipping a page in his book. "Out of seven billion people, not even four hundred have magic." Jordan just gave me a confused look as if he couldn't understand how it was shocking to me. "How do you know how many people are around? Did you count me as a magician or a warlock? What about the Sons and Daughters?"

"Not all the members of those two orders are magic users. A growing number aren't. You ought to remember that while the Daughters are somewhat of a judicial body for magic users, they are both just orders dedicated to hunting the more complicated cases of demons and rogues," he explained. I must have still looked skeptical as he let out a short laugh and added, "You can trust me. I'm powerful enough I can keep track. Magic users aren't so difficult to sense."

"Right." I took another bite. "You're superhuman."

Jordan smirked. "Wizard."

"Do all wizards blur in photographs?" I asked wanting to get him knocked down a peg or two, but he just continued munching on his fries with this know-it-all sort of face. "Fine, then let's talk about the fact Giuseppe summoned a bunch of hellhounds."

"Hellhounds? Oh, the Yeth. It wasn't terribly unusual. They travel in packs anyways. More organized than Baoht but less so than Evoca." Jordan reached forward for a tall, steaming drink. "You drink coffee, right?" He passed me a like-sized cup.

"Oh, thanks. How do they manage to summon multiple demons? If they're dealing with their soul, they should only be getting one, right?" I pointed out only to have Jordan roll his eyes.

"Parceling of the soul is one of the oldest tricks in the book. Most lower-level demons would be killed by their own kind if they had a full soul right out. Too obvious of a jump in power—they are sneaky. Hoarding power bit by bit to try to get to a higher rung, so it isn't hard to give them a section and bring more demons into the deal. The problem comes with the devaluing of their soul. If all four have only half their soul each left, they have only two souls with which to lure Mammon," Jordan explained to me.

"He's the sort with a hefty price tag then?"

Setting his drink down on the table, he said, "They need a fifth without any sold parts. Three soul minimum with Mammon, and he has the power to back it up. You promise three and he will get them, often sooner than you'd think."

"So, their souls go dark when they parcel them?" I stirred more sugar into my coffee until it was almost more sugar than espresso. It had been a while since I had last enjoyed a good quality coffee divested of all actual taste by raw sugar.

"They go dark when they summon demons. The summoning makes their souls dark enough so Mammon can consume them. The deal is implicit with the summoning. There are always rules," Jordan replied.

"Why five though? Why not three, not previously corrupted souls?" I asked, "Wouldn't it have saved them time?"

"Five person minimum to safely summon the top echelon no matter what with a combined power of at least warlock." He tapped my notebook and waited until I had written down our conversation thus far before continuing. "The more people participating in a summons, the more control you have and the more likely it is the demon won't just break the deal and eat you. If you're summoning demons, your soul is pretty much blackened seven ways to Sunday anyways."

"If the fifth has to have their whole soul to give, why would the fifth agree to join them? It makes no sense," I told him.

"Summoning demons doesn't make sense period." When he realized I wouldn't be satisfied with such a dismissive answer, he continued. "They'll probably convince whoever it is that they don't need his full soul, and maybe they really don't. Only the magic user involved knows the amount of their soul left to fraction out."

"Wow. Trusting no one it is then." Tapping my pen against the pages, I mused aloud, "So the whole First Summoning goes fine because the first demon summoning comes upon an apprentice's soul which is generally untainted."

"And if it is tainted, it's generally better the kid dies there." Jordan had a callousness about him which sometimes rubbed me the wrong way. "We have enough problems without psychopaths entering the magical community."

"Wow, cold."

He shrugged, taking another sip. "Survival of the fittest."

"Still, cold," I mumbled into my coffee. After swallowing a delicious burning gulp of sugar and espresso, I added, "Wouldn't the parents know about the soul beforehand?"

"Which is why some still get out." Jordan shuffled through his pile of papers.

"A laptop would be easier."

He stared blankly at me. "Everyone, everywhere giving up their magic and leaving well enough alone would be easier. This..." He shook the papers. "Is easier to replicate and less expensive."

"You're one of those people who blew up their computer when you got angry with it," I guessed. He raised an eyebrow in response. "Those people totally exist. Probably a bunch of old timers and technophobes blowing up computers and claiming magic interacts poorly with technology."

"I grew up in the eighties. Computers weren't big then."

This time it was my turn to raise an eyebrow or squint trying. "The Commodore 64 came out in the early eighties."

"Spending six hundred dollars on a computer wasn't actually a high priority." Jordan smirked. "Now stop twitching and give up on the eyebrow. We need to ward your dorm." He set a knife, a piece of chalk, and some white paint on the table between us. "Runes ward—these runes..." He set a bookmark covered in what looked like random lines in front of me. "These five runes in this pattern repeated around an opening will protect you. First, you carve." he demonstrated on the end of the table. "Then you chalk and then paint." He followed his instructions, though the paint stood out against the plain wood. "White—right?"

"White? Oh, yeah around the doors and windows the walls are white," I confirmed, and he pushed everything toward me. "Won't I get in trouble for this?"

"If the color doesn't match enough for it to blend in or look like a repair, text me, and I'll get you a better match," Jordan offered before turning back to what he had been doing. I traced a finger over the runes. They seemed familiar.

"These are the same runes as the store, aren't they?" Jordan nodded, and I continued to trace them. "So... the ruins are Norse, right? It doesn't look Greek or Latin."

"Eiwaz, Mannaz, Hagalaz, Ansuz, and Dagaz," Jordan explained as he pointed to each one. "They come from the Norse alphabet. Eiwaz..." He pointed to the first rune which was a straight line a smaller line coming off the top and bottom. The line coming off the top was slightly down tilted and went from the top point of the vertical line forward. The line coming off the bottom was slightly up tilted and went from the bottom point of the vertical line backwards. "Is a protective rune which, in this position, references Yggdrasil, the tree of life in Nordic legend. If you have somebody who knows what they're doing, Eiwaz will always be present and first. Mannaz represents mankind." The rune sort of looked like an 'M' with an hourglass at the top area. He pointed to the next which was like an 'N' with a second diagonal line over the first. "Hagalaz represents the dramatic change, the salvation available to those who enter into the covenant and the damnation to those who don't. Ansuz represents God, and Dagaz always ends the rune protection. It symbolizes a return to balance."

The rune Ansuz was a vertical line with two diagonal lines. Both lines were tilted downwards and forward. One came off the middle and the other off the top. Dagaz looked like an hourglass had fallen onto its side. Honestly, it was way too similar to the whole infinity symbol protection thing. Jordan placed four photographs on the table, and I put away the supplies knowing I would have to wait until Tyson was out of the room; otherwise, he would think I was absolutely insane. Zipping my bag back up, I studied the pictures.

"These are the four?" I looked over Rio, Madrid, a guy I had to assume was Henry Blake, and Giuseppe. "Why didn't Blake come last night?"

"He's new. Giuseppe wanted to send a message, so he came. Rio and Madrid were sent to recruit Max. Blake wasn't necessary then. You, however, ought to know who to look out for." Jordan pointed to the picture of the swept back hair. The color was an odd sort of brown. His eyes were indiscernible from the picture, either hazel or some mixture of green and blue. His nose was narrow and tilted at the bottom like it had been broken a few times, and he was impeccably dressed in a suit I would have bet was worth more than all my clothes put together.

"Henry Blake—okay, so put runes on and avoid these four. Got it, now how about some magic," I said rubbing my hands together.

Jordan stood, clearing away the remainders of his meal accept for the drink. The remainders went in the trash, and the cup went on the counter. Before he vanished into the back area, he called, "Eat—then magic."

The whole free food wonderfulness kept me from arguing. I didn't want to discourage what I found to be an awesome trend forming. When my burger was safely in my stomach, I took the fries still in the white box and headed around the store. The store was still empty which left me wondering how the business was getting by. There wasn't a speck of dust on anything, and I noticed a few areas had a few less volumes, so either Jordan kicked everybody out before I came, or I just had fantastic timing. I'd like to think the second, but more likely than not, probably the first. Jordan came around the corner with a piece of paper in hand and tugged a book from the shelf. He went along and pulled two more before turning to me.

"Don't touch the books with those fingers," Jordan commanded.

He vanished amongst the shelves. Sitting back, I ate my fries and spun cyclones. The winds meandered down the aisles then melded back into the rest of the air. Moving from the table, I chewed my fries walking from shelf to shelf. When I reached the one Jordan had turned down, I slid down leaning against the side.

"Aren't there any books about magic?" I called out knowing wherever he was, Jordan would hear me.

From across the paper forest, he answered, "All books are about magic; you just need to find out what you can and cannot do." He reappeared around a corner empty-handed. "As a warlock, you've got limits. You wouldn't be able to warp-fold, speak in tongues, or alter your internal make-up. No one can heal, but some wizards can manage to slightly alter their chemistry. You won't be able to do it."

"Could I make a golem?"

Jordan laughed. "You could, but it would just be an extension of your will. If you decide to, demons often utilize them for protection against the sun. It's rather fallen out of practice."

I thought back on all my years of video games, comic books, and fantasy novels. There was a wide array of spells already floating out around the world from the minds of people who—in all likelihood—lacked the capacity to do them.

"Could I produce a protection charm?"

"I bet yours would be a giant squid." Jordan returned leaning against the opposite wall beside the door. "Perhaps if you try hard enough."

I shut the container and pushed it aside. "You're kidding, right? You said magic was basically the worst thing ever, but how can it be bad if I can do something so amazing most people only dream of?"

"You can't build a spacecraft, split continents, or kill someone with a single thought. There's no immediate death spell, though might be simpler—kinder even—but every life form has a will of its own, and magic can only do so much." He sank down to sit across from me. "You can't force your will on another—mortal or magic user. Mortals won't notice, and magic users would kill you for the attempt. Magic is a force of will—partially yours, partially its own—and can sway others only as much as you could without it."

"There's plenty of people who talk others into doing things."

Jordan paused and looked at me carefully as if considering the weight of what I was asking before he said, "Can you?"

"No, but if another magic user could with words, can he with magic?" I pressed.

Jordan shook his head. "He'd use the words, Jon. Magic is a weapon, not a diplomat."

My phone buzzed with a text from Tyson. "Sorry," I mumbled.

"We're done for today. Theory and protection first and think of five spells from your favorite stories you want to try, but for now, go be with your friends." Jordan stood and walked away with an afterthought of, "Don't let magic steal them from you."

I stood slowly, uncertain I wanted to meet the others in the park especially when it was only a bit after five. However, if Jordan was done, there was little I could do to convince him otherwise, so with a wave, I headed out in the storm after putting on my hat and gloves and shoving my backpack over one shoulder. To the dorm and then to the park, my cloth-covered thumbs sent the message to Tyson, and I could almost feel his relief when I didn't blow them off in the affirmative and simple two letter reply I received in return: *OK.*

Nine

Carving the runes into the window wasn't difficult. I had to wait a few days until Monday when I had a break between classes in the middle of the morning while Tyson was stuck in class straight through until three, then weight training with his team until dinner. The wards were simple enough. The shapes were just straight lines, but I knew my life could depend upon them. I carved slowly until the window was completely encased before chalking and painting the lines. When I was done, I stuck my head into the hallway making sure the coast was still clear, and he hadn't gotten out of class early and decided to come back to the dorm. Deciding it was clear, I carved the runes all around. The three sides were easy enough, but there was a rug. I pulled out my phone and rang Jordan.

"Carpet," I informed him. "You didn't think about the carpet."

"To the ninth circle," he swore down the line.

I glared at the carpet. "Invisible ink?"

"You wouldn't be able to tell when or if the warding cracked. Crap, okay— something visible but invisible. Peel up the carpet," he ordered, and I sat on my floor glaring at empty space and imagining it was his face.

"'Cause ripping up a rug won't have financial ramifications."

"Chalk and paint beneath the carpet and seal it back down. I'm sure you'll do fine." Then the phone clicked as he hung up.

I threw my phone on my bed knowing it wouldn't be justified to throw it against the wall simply for transmitting Jordan's stupidity. I grabbed the edge of the carpet where it met the hall carpet and pulled up, slowly peeling it back and revealing the cement underneath. The carpet went inch by inch so slowly it took over an hour to get it back far enough to be in line with the rest of the wards. I glanced nervously at the clock. Tyson wouldn't be back for a good while, but I had class in less than an hour. It wasn't too far, and I hadn't missed one yet, but we were only a month into the semester. Moreover—because there was always one of those—there was a test today.

The wards had to be done now. I manipulated the air and levied the carpet up and back enough to get to the line for the wards. Chalking those around the frame, I quickly drew them across the floor and grabbed the paint. Only halfway through the part beneath the carpet, the thought hit me. The paint would have to be dried. The normal way because magic could ruin wards, and I'd already risked it by using air to lift the carpet. Completing the paint, I sat down at my desk by the window and waited. The wards were completed around the door, so it was just a matter of hoping they dried in time. Then I noticed a speck outside my window.

I glared at the spider weaving its web from my desk. I liked to think I wasn't afraid of them. After all, spiders were tiny and fragile beneath a boot, but there was something just not comforting about one making a web in my window. Especially knowing I'd forget and open the window letting the arachnid the size of my thumb inside. The best idea—because it was the only one I could manage—was to flick it off the screen before it realized there was a whole at the bottom. I cracked the window. The spider went still. I pushed up the window and flicked the spider. It went flying and whooshed right back in through the screen and gap in a swirl of wings and weirder things until a demon stood before me in a shape of a pocket-sized Giuseppe.

"It is rude to make a wizard wait," he informed me.

"I let you in when I meant to," I lied. "A wizard does not open a window late or early. He opens it precisely when he means to do so."

"You are not a wizard. You are a warlock," he pointed out and sat down on the edge of my laptop.

I shrugged, sitting on my bed trying to maintain a façade of aloofness I wasn't feeling. He crossed his tiny demon legs and smiled at me with his tiny demon face. There was a demon in my room. I had been dumb enough to let it in because I couldn't be smart and realize a little fire or wind would have gotten rid of a spider. I swore to never badmouth any literary wizard for fighting with fists again.

He watched me and I stared horrified back. This was absolutely absurd; the spider was a demon on my desk in the shape of Giuseppe. Smiling slyly, he gestured toward my desk chair. The list of what was wrong with this situation was growing longer the more I had time to think about it. I didn't want to take my eyes off of him, but I only had so much time before my roommate came back, and I didn't want to have to explain why I was talking to whatever he would end up interpreting Giuseppe's demon miniature as.

"Aren't you going to offer me a beverage?" Giuseppe's voice was thick with an accent I was left to assume was Italian; however, there was a twist around the words which didn't seem quite normal.

The mini-fridge under my bed hummed all the louder. The jerk probably manipulated the airwaves to point out he knew I'd have to turn my back on him if I were to offer the demon anything. I wasn't going to do so. Offering a demon a drink was kind of the last thing I wanted to do in this situation. Anyways, my cups were totally twice the size of the homunculus. My brain rejected the word even though the definition of a small, proportional human worked if I completely ignored the fact the humanoid was, in fact, a demon. Trying hard to maintain concentration, I sought for a response, and all I had was the distressing thought I didn't even own a box of matches. Girls might sneak in candles, but I didn't even have a random lighter. My lack of pyromania had finally come around to bite me.

"You came in uninvited," I ventured, betting the phrase would do little to assist my case.

Mini-Giuseppe snorted and tapped his cane. A small bistro style table materialized in front of him with a saucer and cup of coffee. "You opened the window."

"To get rid of the spider."

"Which you did." He nodded with a smile, taking a sip of the foamed cup. Licking his lips, he sighed. "This city isn't the best for cappuccinos, but there is always one café."

"How are you even doing this?" Studying the table and coffee, I tried to determine which café, but Rochester has a coffee shop every twenty to forty feet. "Are you somewhere drinking coffee? Or is this just to amuse you?"

"This demon is under my control for a portion of my soul smaller than you might comprehend. It does not think or function on its own, but maintains itself with a small section. The demon exists placing only its survival above my commands. There isn't truly a deal because this demon..." The tiny Giuseppe gestured at his impeccable suit. "Could not fathom such. It is nothing more than a speck of celestial dust which once darkened some fool's doorway. However, it acts splendidly as a mirror for communication."

"So your answer is a yes."

"To what question?" he returned with another sip.

Holding in all the frustration building since tracking Jordan down, I took a deep breath before continuing. "Why are you here?"

"It wasn't one of your questions."

"It is now."

He clucked his tongue and shook his head. "Terribly rude—I don't see how you've managed so long."

"So long? I've only been doing this for like a month—maybe two tops." I surged forward glaring at the little insignificant speck sitting on my laptop like he owned the place. Stupid little bistro chair.

He set his cup down on its saucer and shifted in his seat, moving the crossed leg back down and the opposite over. "I would think you were lying if you weren't so terribly naïve."

I shrugged. "I saw Jordan beat up a demon; it was cool, and now, here I am."

"Obviously you've made grave mistakes in your life making such hurried decisions. Well then." He smiled, leaning forward. "We have more to speak on than I previously believed. How well do you know Jordan?"

"I met him like a month ago," I admitted with a shrug. Unable to leave it there, my sarcasm revved up. "It was a dark alley, one thing led to another. It was terribly romantic."

His eyes narrowed, and the smile faded into a neutral face. "Before I waste my time on you and your poorly chosen capacity to jump into messes you ought not leap into, answer me this: did it ever cross your mind you're fighting for the wrong side?"

"Against demons." I frowned. "Not likely."

"Demons might be the vessel we are using; however, the use of them does not define any one side. There have been plenty of evil mortals who have not used demons to venture terrible darkness upon the world. There are just as many magic users who have likewise avoided the spawn of Hell, yet they are no gentler in their destructive ways," Giuseppe's miniature explained slowly. If his face hadn't already told me he thought I was an idiot, his tone would leave nothing to my imagination.

"I don't think demons are like guns. Some bits, no matter how they're used, are just plain evil. You know, considering they have their own motives and generally not nice ones," I retorted with my best naïve-dingus smile.

Giuseppe's tiny little doppelganger—seriously, how many ways could this be described without giving the false impression of him actually being here?—stood and swaggered toward me. The table and what remained of his coffee faded with each step away from them. He twirled a fedora out of nowhere and stuck it on his little, tiny demonic head. Leaning on his cane, he glared up at me with his scrunched up olive-toned face, and blue eyes that glowed a dark red beneath the façade of humanity.

He raised his hand, wagging a finger at me. "The will of a demon is as great or as small as their void. If you have any skill, the will isn't what matters."

"Magic has a will."

"Magic is a tool."

"Tools don't have opinions."

"I believe modern expression tells otherwise."

I was eighteen—give me a break. "You're a tool."

"Everyone is somebody's tool." The demon smiled, and the grin blurred out too far, showing a bit of the demon underneath the whole cloak of Giuseppe. I couldn't help but wonder if it was the demon winking at me. Like it was pointing out Giuseppe was the real dimwit. He threw up his hands. "I can see this conversation has rounded. Five against one isn't fantastic odds. You're untrained—untested. Do you think Jordan will protect you when the time comes? He's the sort to only defend himself. Even if you are too close-minded to rationalize the benefits of demons, you truly need to question whether or not the team you've chosen will have your back."

"I think I'll make do."

He leaned back on his heels. "Make do? Hardly! You can't even keep a demon out of your dorm."

Shoving my hands into my pockets, I felt the distinctive shape of a rave ring from the night before. I slipped my finger into it and flicked the switch slamming my hand on the desk. The demon wasn't there, but there hadn't been much resistance, so I slowly lifted my hand. Mini-Giuseppe was gone. I glanced around and caught him standing on the window sill.

"Poor form." He tapped his tiny cane, and a spider crawled out. "The void, my uneducated friend, never left the web." The spider's legs gestured vaguely around a small dark spot the size of a pin's head.

"It's sunny. The void should have burned off naturally," I replied staring at the spot. The spider crawled closer and pulled aside some spider silk. "The heat then!"

"It's thirty degrees out, Jon. The silk blocked the sun." The spider shook, but moved aside letting the sun hit the void for a moment before slipping through with a final opinion. "What is he teaching you if you can't even spot a void?"

The spider was back in Hell, and I spent the rest of the time when I should have been studying making sure my room was void free to prevent a demon from entering. There was a lot of fire manipulation, flashlights, and a desperate call to Jordan. I dialed without ever looking down. The phone rang twice before a click, and I was certain Jordan had just rejected my call until his voice came over the line.

"What?" Irritable at his best.

"Giuseppe sent a demon to my dorm. You said the wards would keep them out," I accused as my fingers traced over the invisible ink where I had marked the sill and frame keeping the demons out, or so I had thought.

The phone went dead quiet for a long pause. For a moment, I considered whether or not he had lost the connection or simply hung up on me then he said, "You opened the window."

"Of course I opened the window. It was a spider! It's getting nicer out! Sort of! I didn't want it on my window! I thought opening it wouldn't matter. Open or closed, the wards are still there," I retorted. "What do I do? If I can't tell a demon apart from a bug, how am going to survive being a wizard? I'm the sidekick in my own life—even before you showed up—I'm going to end up getting splattered. Oh, my mom's going to kill me. I promised her I would be careful!"

I wasn't going to add in I promised her I wouldn't put too much faith in Jordan because it went without saying. Whatever relationship Jordan had with my dad, it didn't translate well with my mom; otherwise, I think he would have been invited to Christmas dinner or Thanksgiving at least once. The pause repeated the same as before except this time it was followed by a click and a dial tone. Swearing had never been something I found useful, but suddenly, colorful words became the best way I could think of to release the amount of stress Giuseppe had piled on with his ventriloquist demon puppet show.

One slow knock rolled over my room. I turned and yanked open my door to get smacked upside the back of the head as Jordan walked in scolding me. "Never open the door without checking!"

"I checked with the window, and the spider turned out to be a demon anyways," I griped rubbing at the back of my head. Sitting down on my bed, I glowered as Jordan shut the door and pushed his aura to encompass the entire room.

"You're lucky," he said turning to me. "He didn't leave a hook behind."

"I already looked for hooks and heated the entire room. Just because I opened a window does not mean I'm incompetent as a warlock." I quickly kicked my backpack and dirty laundry under the bed between my mini-fridge and the storage boxes. Jordan watched me with this dry unimpressed expression. "What?"

Jordan shook his head. "If you open a ward, it isn't warded intrinsically." He tapped the wards beneath the window and they glowed. "You have to slip them a bit of power."

"But magic is from Hell. Magic wants to get back to Hell," I quoted the lesson a bit less than verbatim, but the point was still intact. "How exactly does magic maintain anything? You said the wards were the only bits not out to get me."

"You aren't using magic directly." He glowed—the harsh outline of his soul showing. "You use a bit of your soul. If you aren't completely corrupted, a pin point of your soul could power wards for days."

"I thought soul didn't grow back."

Jordan rolled his eyes. "The wards borrow the bit, but you can get it back."

The glow went into the wards, which became visible. He lifted his hand, and the runes remained lit. Jordan tapped the wards twice in quick time; they faded from view, and the light sunk into his fingertips before dispersing amongst his person. Turning, Jordan took a step toward the door, stopping and changing direction toward my bureau in the corner of the room. On the top of the standard issue, college, five-drawer dresser was a picture of my mom and me. She had insisted I have at least one picture of her somewhere obvious, so I could look at her face and think of how upset she would be if I did something stupid.

The photograph was of my sixteenth birthday. The coast had been hit by a gigantic ice storm no one could explain, but there hadn't been any damage despite all the warnings blaring across the radio and television stations. We both stood in winter jackets at our house where everything was covered in a thin layer of ice and snow. The small tree in our front yard we planted when we first moved in when I was just starting school looked like the white tree of Gondor. I had always loved J.R.R. Tolkien's books and the movies, so when I had woken up on my birthday and seen it, I had been absurdly excited.

Jordan studied the photograph. His hand hovered at the edge as if he wanted to pick the frame up but wasn't certain doing so was the best idea. Walking over to his side, I picked up the picture and held it out to him. "Sixteenth birthday—it was the best day. School got closed because of the ice."

"Your mother looks the same as she did the day I met her," Jordan whispered.

I glanced down at my mom's face. I had never met Jordan before, but my mom had certainly changed from the older photographs of her we had up in our living room. Not in a bad way, just the sort of change which happens working two jobs and then one intense job while raising a kid as a single mother. Jordan gently took the picture from my hand. He gazed down with an indecipherable expression on his face. After a moment, he returned the picture back to the top of my dresser looking at me like a bug under a magnifying glass.

"Do you have a picture of my dad?" I asked. Jordan was on the edge of sentimental, so the time was the best it would ever be to push. "We don't have anything with him in it."

"No. Your father wasn't fond of cameras," Jordan replied. He headed toward the door. Stepping into the hallway, he turned. "Do you even know your dad's name?"

The question was loaded. It was easy enough to tell by the narrowing of his eyes and tenseness in his jaw. I shrugged. "Yeah, Jokul Van der Berg. They weren't ever officially married, so my mom put her last name down on the birth certificate."

"You've got your dad's name on your birth certificate?" Jordan looked at me like he wasn't sure if I even could properly confirm what he was asking.

I nodded. "Yeah, I've seen it, but I've just got her last name listed."

"Have you ever looked up the name on the internet to find him?" Jordan acted like what he was asking was off-hand, but he watched me too carefully for it to be.

"Sure, I did it a lot when I was a kid. It always said I spelled the name wrong."

Jordan pulled super glue out and squirted it along the floor then pushed the carpet down with a toe. "Your life is a series of poorly timed ideas."

"Hey, it was good timing; otherwise, the demon could have gotten in on its own," I pointed out, but it was obviously not the right thing to say.

"This has become too big of a risk," Jordan said.

My heart sank in my chest. "What? No, it's not a risk. It was probably a onetime thing to scare me off."

"They'll target you as long as you're involved. The best we can do is to declare you're a neutral party and continue your training without you getting involved any further with them or the summoning." Jordan leaned against the door frame.

I shrugged. "Fine, neutral party. Now, when do you want to meet up for training?"

"Next week—Sunday at two," Jordan replied and stepped back from the door into the hallway. "If you see any of them, you will immediately announce you're no longer a party to the hunt. They might still attack."

"It was a onetime thing," I whispered.

I didn't know how to convince him I wouldn't be so stupid again. There was nothing I could think of to reason with him. I'd never been the best with words, but I had thought we'd had an understanding. I wanted this more than I'd wanted anything.

Jordan shook his head slowly. "Weekly sessions only, Jon. Once a week until this is done, and don't come to the shop otherwise."

My fists clenched at my side. "Nothing actually happened. Why are you being so weird about it?" Jordan shook his head again and walked away. I stormed after him. "I've got the amulet. I was fine. You said demons couldn't touch me until my first summoning, so I wasn't even in danger."

Jordan rounded on me. His eyes were narrowed in a fierce glare. "Of Hell, Jon. You have no danger of going to Hell. Maybe demons on the street will be deterred, but if Giuseppe had ordered the demon to kill you, it would have done so regardless of where your soul would go. You are not trained enough to protect yourself if a demon takes interest."

"This is exactly why only training once in a week is pointless! I need to learn more not less," I argued.

Resting his face in his hand, Jordan sighed. "I made a promise to keep you safe, and I have a job to do. Once a week—text me if this happens again."

He strode away and slammed the door to the stairs behind him. I stood defeated in the hallway, uncertain of what I could do or say to change his mind. In the end, I turned back around and closed my door. Sitting at my desk, I stared at the space where Giuseppe's demon doppelganger had sat. It was only when my eyes slid to my clock I realized my class started in three minutes. Grabbing my backpack, I ran out of the door.

Ten

Protection Charm
~~Turning a pen into a sword~~ Enchanting objects
Plasma energy ~~ball~~ control
~~Alchemy, stuff into gold~~
Tracking spell

My list wasn't the best. I kept thinking it could be better, but a week had gone by, and there I was back in the store with Jordan reading over my less than stellar list. He pulled out a pen and crossed out number four completely then altered number two and three before sliding the list back to me.

"Stuff into gold?"

My shoulders sagged. "What? Can't that be done?"

"No." He shook his head, chuckling. "Even enchanting objects is going to be a push. Tracking is simple enough—make skin particles left behind or footprints or scents more prominent. Protection charm—plenty of those from a basic defensive illusion to various shields. Plasma—utilizing lightning is the same as air or water or fire or anything else—elemental manipulation. Enchanting—it's not exactly how magic works."

"So I can't put a spell innately in an object. I mean, what about runes or Rio's tattoos," I pointed out.

Jordan nodded. "Which is why it isn't crossed out. I'll go more into runes, but it wouldn't be what you're thinking. You can't change the core of an object. It's like when you manipulate fire. It's an extension and intensification of heat. Try turning a pen into a sword, and you'd have the most fragile sword in existence."

I stuck the list back in my pocket. "So, we're done until next week right? Or can we do more than one lesson a week? I've been practicing in the empty classrooms around campus. Look!"

I concentrated and made the books on the shelves jump around before lifting the table with the air. Jordan nodded, and I pulled out my new lighter and did a few tricks with fire sending it circling around the room in the shape of a dragon. I didn't expect praise. Jordan wasn't keen on such niceties.

"Books burn, Jon."

I let the fire go out. "Come on—I'm getting better. I've practiced with the wards—even warded my bed."

The last bit got a laugh out of him. "And when was the last time you spent time with your friends?"

"Well, later today, but I eat with them all the time, and we study." I sounded incredibly lame even to my own ears.

"Go, be a mortal for a while. We're done for today. I want you to work on controlling smoke, and don't even try plasma when I'm not there; we'll do it next week. There's a storm on its way, so it'll be easy to disguise. Practice shielding like I taught you." He summoned his protective suit, and I did my best to do the same. I had almost manipulated my shield into a complete body covering, but every once in a while my head sort of got left out. The shield did it again this time, leaving my forehead a target.

"Yeah." I let the shield drop. "I'll work on it. Bye!"

"Be careful," Jordan told me as I raced out the door toward the park to meet up with the guys.

I sent a text to Tyson saying I would be there for football. The plan had been for him and the rest to play against his friend, Gabriel, who went to Rochester Institute of Technology which was locally known as RIT. I had said I'd meet them late originally, so Tyson seemed pretty pleased when he sent a text saying: *swt.* I assumed it meant sweet, but he used a lot more text talk than I had ever, so who knows. I got to the park pretty quickly and headed toward the section where Tyson said he and Joel would be. As I drew nearer, my heart sank.

Henry Blake was the name of a man with a history, but when I saw him sitting on a park bench, I barely recognized him as the guy from the picture. His normally swept back brown hair hung in tattered wisps, and his absurdly expensive suit was burnt around the edges. His black shoes were scuffed. Blake held his head in his hands glowering at the ground while the world moved on around him, and I had no idea how I was supposed to react. There was no telling if Blake knew I was Jordan's apprentice, but if he did, there was a good chance getting as far away from this place as possible was the best idea, but my friends were tossing around a football right in front of the bench. Bailing on them was not an option. I'd made excuse after excuse for weeks to practice in empty classrooms and learn from Jordan. They were good friends, but everyone had a tipping point.

Tyson noticed me and waved me over. I had to take the chance Blake had no idea who I was, and this was all some sort of coincidence. Just because Jordan would have considered him suspicious didn't mean I had to, so off I went across the field to join my friends. Joel flung the football at my face, and I caught it with only slight difficulty before lobbing the ball to Tyson. I was the only non-footballer here. Back in high school, I'd been on the basketball team. The coach wanted me more for my height than anything else. My hand-eye coordination was good. I just didn't always remember to dribble. Carrying the ball was just faster.

"I thought we were playing a pick-up with your buddy from RIT," I said catching the ball from Tyson and passing it along to Joel.

Tyson checked his phone somehow still catching the football when Joel threw it at him. He tucked the ball under his arm, and his thumbs flew across his phone before he shoved it back in his pocket. "Probably just running late."

Before he could throw the ball, Joel pulled out his own phone. "Crap, I got to get to work."

"What? Seriously?" Tyson groused.

Joel gestured at his phone. "Beckah just broke her arm in the cooler, and no one else is available. Sorry, I need the hours." He zipped his sweater and took off.

"What now?" I asked, turning to Tyson who glared in Joel's direction. "Are the rest of the guys still coming?"

"One sec." Tyson pulled out the phone, tossing me the ball to hold as he called the RIT crew.

Standing around, I had almost forgotten Blake was lurking until I noticed snowflakes collecting on the ball. By all means, snow in early April wasn't out of the ordinary in Rochester. A bit more so than March snow, but there was precedence if Tyson was to be believed. However, the day had begun in the high forties, and the ball should have been warm enough to melt them quicker. I glanced upwards. The sky was filled with large, nearly black clouds closer to those found in a thunderstorm than a snowstorm.

"Tyson," I called. "Maybe we should reschedule this."

"Why?" Tyson cut himself off and unleashed a long line of expletives. Pulling his hood over his head, Tyson reached out for the ball, and I tossed it to him. "Let's get back to the dorms. Seriously, I swear someone's out to ruin my day."

"No waffle mix left in the dining center?"

Tyson scowled. "Stupid spring sports."

"Yeah, no one should get up before eleven on a weekend," I agreed, walking alongside back to our dorm. The fact I had been up and out before seven a good amount of mornings this past month wasn't something I was going to bring up. I had been considerate enough in doing so he had no reason to either. The rave was a lesson well learned.

"I swear they just use it all up before we get there because we're the football team. It's such crap." He tossed the ball lightly in the air and caught it. "Next fall we're going to make their breakfasts miserable!"

A key mark of a lot of fantasy novels was the sidekick best friend with slightly less extraordinary powers or no extraordinary power at all who was just sort of along for the ride. If I had a choice, Tyson Scott was not the person I'd pick. Mostly because he would totally end up being cooler than me. He'd turn into some sort of Samwise Gamgee beating up monsters with pans. I couldn't handle it considering Jordan had relegated me to assistant status.

Despite knowing Tyson would be awesome, I also kind of wanted to protect him. He was the first best friend I had ever had. We'd clicked. If I could avoid him ever finding out, I would have. Of course, the hope left me rather disappointed when someone tapped me on the shoulder, and that someone turned out to be Henry Blake. Large black circles cradled his eyes. His neatly cut sideburns flared out about his jaw line. He looked like some Civil War aristocrat—silver pocket watch included.

"I don't mean to intrude upon y'all's conversation, but could one of you be implored to give me the hour afore y'all seek shelter from the oncoming squall?" he inquired in a smooth drawl. In between the words, there was a twang which itched against my nerves.

Tyson's eyes trailed over Blake then settled on his shattered wristwatch before flicking up to his pocket watch. "Round three-twenty."

"I was addressing the thaumaturge," Blake retorted. His eyes slid to Tyson. "Not his pet."

Tyson shoved the football into my chest, pushing me aside. "Excuse you?"

"Come on, Tyson. He's obviously deranged." I gestured at Blake's burnt clothes.

Blake sneered as his fingers fluttered over the edges. "Courtesy of your master, boy."

And any chance of Tyson not going off the rails was gone. He was born and raised in Rochester. This was the city of Frederick Douglass and Susan B. Anthony as he liked to remind me. Focusing in pre-law, Tyson had academic and sports scholarships easing his way to his dream job at a top international women's rights organization. He thrived on standing up to bigots. Whether I liked it or not, Blake had pushed all the right buttons to keep Tyson's attention.

"This is a free county. No one here has a master, and no one keeps another human as a pet," Tyson informed Blake. "I suggest you back off."

Blake looked pretty far from amused around the eyes, but he smiled like this was his new favorite game. "Your kind..." I cringed; I physically cringed. "Don't deserve our protection. You're headed south anyways. We ought to send you in style."

I grabbed Tyson's arm feeling a bit more like a sidekick than I thought I should, given the circumstances. Blake was riling Tyson, but this was all a play for a legitimate reason to attack with whatever demon he had on retainer.

"Come on, Ty, this guy is just trying to cause trouble. Let's get back to the dorm." I pushed, but Tyson was a good fifty pounds heavier than me, and every ounce was muscle.

"This is a city of progress. The close-minded have no right—"

"If you believe in rights for all, the close-minded have every right." Blake laughed. "Politics always runs in such wide courses when the reality remains those who you want to silence with your exclamations are the representatives of your failures. A city of progress has all—a city of progress would permit all vileness you wish to censure from the population."

"I swear this is not going to end well for anybody. I am a neutral party!" I proclaimed, but I was on the periphery at this point. "Seriously, side kicked even here?"

"Respect for all is progress!"

"Respect is earned!"

"We are all endowed with the same basic liberties," Tyson returned the volley.

And Blake knocked it back. "This government does not rule the world. The world has no unification—no basic liberties. You cannot tame them with words! Imperialism is your legacy with those proclamations!"

"Anyone curious why he didn't just use his pocket watch?" I asked, but they ignored me.

Reaching forward, Blake either was too engrossed in the argument or didn't care as I pulled it out of his pocket. Clicking the button on the top to open it, I frowned. A woman's picture was on one side. She was pretty though not someone who would

be considered traditionally beautiful. Her soulful brown eyes
were delicately slanted above wide cheekbones. Her nose was a
little wide, and she had crooked teeth. On the other side of the
watch where the clock should have been was a small dark circle. I
thought the circle was paper at first then the reality hit me as did
Tyson's elbow.

"Are you even paying attention to this insult to the idea of a
human being?" Tyson accused.

"I—" I gestured vaguely at the pocket watch, and the void
nestled inside, but Blake pulled it back, closing it.

"Your grandmother's Creole," Tyson reminded me.

I kept my eyes on Blake; then, sighing, I grumbled, "The last
thing my grandmother said to me back when I was six was I was
an illegitimate spawn born of sinful fornication and wouldn't get
a cent from their estate."

"As a man of mixed race—" Tyson tried again, but Blake was
focusing again, and it was dangerous when my attention was
getting split.

"Your great-grandfather was from the Netherlands," I retorted. "The only reason I know about your great-grandfather and
you know about my grandparents was because of stupid freshman
weekend."

"First year orientation was the best! We bonded." He gestured between us.

I had to admit, "Yeah, but..." I turned my attention back to
Blake who was fiddling with the watch. "I've got enough distance
to know when someone's just playing Devil's advocate to screw
with me."

"Temperature is dropping rather quickly," Blake noted idly.

Tyson shivered. "Fine, come on."

He turned to leave, and I followed a few steps behind keeping my eyes on Blake who simply smiled. While Tyson's back was
turned, the smile tore up further into his face into a giant,
gruesome mockery of the Cheshire Cat with the triangle teeth
and black void of a throat from the movies. Tyson glanced back,
and the demon had once against resumed the ruse of Blake's
human face.

"The guy's a freak," Tyson muttered, and we crossed the street.

"Yeah." I nodded and quickly sent a text to Jordan. I got a one-word reply in response—*Mugwærm.*

I sounded the word out in my mind all the while wondering how he got the weird smashed together A and E symbol on his phone. I glimpsed back over my shoulder, but the demon—Mugwærm—was out of sight. Stuffing my phone back in my pocket, I trudged the rest of the way back to my dorm room knowing Tyson would rant off and on for hours once we got there. My mind, however, was on the threat the rogues had just been issued. Henry Blake knew who I was and was watching me with some of the demons on his retainer. Neutral party or not—I was irrevocably involved.

Eleven

If I had thought Jordan would be concerned for my well-being or let me go to the shop more often, I was sorely mistaken. I went after class on Tuesday and was promptly kicked out from the surprisingly full shop with nothing but a book on shielding spells and runes to reinforce protection on clothing. Spring had finally arrived; though considering it had been only a week since the last snow fall, by the next Sunday I didn't have high hopes. I came to the shop a bit early wearing my spring jacket. All the pockets were inscribed with runes in permanent marker as were the hems around the arms, wrists, waist, zipper, and collar. From the outside, it looked normal, but inside it was a mess of black Norse characters.

The day was in the fifties. Rochester was climbing back toward normal for the season, and I hadn't seen hide or hair of the rogues. I hadn't exactly gone out and about looking for them. The store was once again empty, and Jordan was sewing something into the inner edge of a black leather jacket. The thread was well-matched, but the cotton twine stood out despite his best attempts. They were runes.

"Nice jacket. I thought you already had runes on everything," I said, and he shook his head concentrating on the stitches.

"My jacket's hanging up. This is for you," he informed me.

I unzipped my jacket and displayed the runes. "But, I'm good. See?"

Jordan glanced up. Catching sight of my runes, he put the needle down. "Permanent marker?"

"Yeah?"

"Workable—this was your father's." He knotted the edge and cut the thread. "I reinforced the wards. It's fire proof, so magical or not these threads won't fail."

"Neither will my permanent marker," I replied, but already I was reaching out with grabby hands for the jacket. "My dad's? Wow, so he was my size." I slid the jacket on and ran my hands over the leather. The weight was more than what I was accustomed to, but it hardly mattered. It was my dad's.

"If it fits, keep it. I've had it for a while now, and I'm sure he'd be happy to know you got it. If I remember correctly, the jacket was what got him your mother," Jordan told me.

I couldn't help myself; I floated up a few inches off the ground in pure excitement. "Take a picture!" I shoved my cell phone in his hand and willed myself to the ground. "I bet I look so cool!"

I did my best to stop the grin spreading across my face as he snapped a few shots then handed it back to me. I flipped through and decided on the best one and sent it to my mom. When my phone confirmed the picture had been sent, a bit of guilt settled in. I hadn't talked to my mom since I had gotten started with this whole training affair. We'd texted a bit. She knew I was independent, and I hadn't been the sort to call more than once a month or even less anyways, but the realization settled she probably would want more updates on what was going on than I had given her, so I sent a follow-up text asking if we could talk tonight.

"Put the phone away," Jordan said putting on his own dark brown, leather coat. "We've got a job to do."

"I thought I wasn't involved in the hunt," I pointed out, watching the door close behind me.

Jordan shrugged as he walked down the steps. "They're watching you. No point in being thick."

As we passed through the door, I glanced back, and there was the ram's skull where the normal knob had been. It glinted in the afternoon light in an almost taunting manner like a small child who smugly thought he had gotten away with staying up late despite his mother's presence at his doorway. I pulled my tired eyes away and quickened my pace to catch up to Jordan. Slowly, the streets we passed filled with people: ordinary people. They were the sort of people who ignored you, bumped into you, or just smiled politely as they passed. Those people had never seen or even thought of demons as more than a passing midnight fancy over a good gothic horror. It was odd to think about it. I had seen odd things, magical things, all my life, but I had never felt so much like the outsider than I felt like now. When I walked beside Jordan, a bit behind him to be honest because he walked Kenyan Olympic gold medalist fast, it was like an invisibility cloak had just covered me.

It was an hour into walking when I couldn't keep quiet any longer. "Don't you have a car or something? We'd be able to cross more distance in a car."

"Cars have numerous shadows in which demons can hook themselves, too risky," he gruffly replied, and I had the feeling I'd have to be an idiot to question it.

"You said you had another motorcycle. Why don't we use it?"

"We're not going long distance. We're patrolling," he retorted.

The streets I had been familiar with became less the ones I remembered and more the streets I had avoided going down. People in business suits and people with cardboard signs who sat in the corner of stairwells and stoops became the norm. Everything seemed to suggest nothing was out of the ordinary, which was why the first time I saw an upper level demon was so calmly, so horrifyingly stuck in my mind. He walked down the street as though it was all just too cliché. Probably was. He had witnessed thousands of human lives and cities simply come and go within a breath. We were nothing to him. We were at most tiny insects in comparison to the length of his eternity.

His strides were long and smooth, and his hands were hidden in the depths of his black military jacket's pockets. He wore a black, button-up dress shirt and tailored slacks. The wind whipped around, rattling the coins around his neck on a box-linked chain. They weren't something I expected to see. Tiny little coins and thicker amulets jingled together like beacons of honor around his neck. The amulet lying against my skin burned, and I couldn't look away from his cold face. His skin was a rich olive. Black hair was spiraled and half-slicked back off his face. His eyes twinkled as they traced those around him, coloring the world in cruel auburn. His mouth opened as his tongue traced his teeth in a menacing manner while he observed the people as if they were steaks with legs.

I wanted nothing more than to turn the other way and get as quickly as possible out of Dodge, but Jordan did not stop or slow down. He didn't glance at the freak of nature coming our way. He just continued as though nobody was there at all. Jordan turned his head; the demon turned his. They looked directly at each other in this epic manner like when the hero and villain first cross each other's paths. We have entered the moment when hands twitch over the guns waiting in hip holsters. Jordan's gaze was level while the demon looked down from his six foot height. A smirk pulled at the demon's lips, and his left hand came from his pocket. The thumb caught the edge of the chain and lifted it, so the coins clinked together as he raised an eyebrow and tilted his head. His eyes flickered. Age and absence like nothing I had ever seen before loomed out behind him as far as my eyes could see. I knew something big was happening when I saw his void. The city vanished behind a dark hole which threatened to swallow us whole. Jordan shrugged, unimpressed. The demon suddenly squinted and his void shrunk, but I could only guess at what had caused it. Betting he was the source, I squinted and looked at Jordan, but as soon as I did, the light shifted out of my view.

The instant came as they were about to walk past each other. Jordan leaned slightly toward the demon and whispered, "Say hello to Daddy for me." He reached out and yanked the coins off of the demon's necklace. In a tiny moment as the chain broke, the demon's eyes widened then narrowed in an unspoken threat. Before anything else could occur, the demon's void and the light of Jordan's soul collided. I didn't see the collision. I guess I blinked. The demon was there one moment, and in the next, he was gone.

"Which demon was it?" I asked as I looked around in shock. No one had noticed.

"Mammon." Jordan shook his head in disgust as he looked at the coins. "These are wards of protection. They're meant for innocents—for children; the only way he could have these would be if he killed an entire magical line." He shoved them in the inner pocket of his jacket and stormed onwards. "He'll be back."

"Didn't seem so strong," I commented idly, and Jordan turned to face me.

"I didn't banish him, Jon," he said. "He left because of a deal I have with his father. If his father knew he was on Earth..." He smirked slightly, and I got the idea of just what the Devil would do. "Mammon will be back, and he certainly won't be any worse for wear after a round of intimidation. You would do well to remember: Orpheus will do everything he can to stay in Hell; Berith will do anything to stay on Earth; and Mammon—he's rather good at biding his time in either place. If you're willing to call the Devil on him, he'll bow out almost every time."

"If he's so strong, couldn't he have just killed you? I mean, he killed all those people." I gestured toward where he had put the necklace, and Jordan frowned.

"Most people would rather die than summon up the Devil's interest. For me, it's a bit too late. For you..." Jordan looked around and then walked ahead as he called over his shoulder, "Blame your father for the interest he accumulated over his years."

I had the horrible feeling perhaps those people might have had the right idea. I didn't ever want to come face to face or even touch the Devil with a thirty-nine and a half foot pole, but something stuck out in my mind.

"Wait, if Mammon is supposed to stay in Hell, then how can he be summoned by Giuseppe and his crew?" I asked. "Why does his father want him down under anyway?"

"Mammon has a habit of catching the wrong sort of attention. Demons aren't the only ones playing the field. As for a summoning, well, it's out of Mammon's hands. If he is summoned properly with the correct sacrifice, he must come." Jordan sighed running his fingers along the coins. "If we can't beat the summoning, killing him—permanently—will earn everyone involved the attention of the most ruthless creature in all of Hell."

"Lucifer?"

"Lilith," he replied.

I recoiled. "You're kidding. At least tell me her story isn't what I think it is. She seriously didn't get sent to Hell for refusing to subjugate herself to Adam."

Running a hand through his hair, Jordan frowned. "Yes and no."

"How can it be both? She was either punished for using the free will she was given, or she was sent down for some other reason." I had never been the religious sort. The fact my mother and I didn't regularly attend service had been a huge splitting point with my grandparents, but I had too many questions, and my mother never enjoyed the crowds.

"According to Lilith, she was sent southwards after she killed Eve."

My eyes narrowed. "Eve came after Lilith."

"Lilith—supposedly—agreed to disagree with Adam; God said, 'whatever,' and promised to make them both their own partners. Adam got Eve, and Lilith rejected every single attempt," Jordan explained. "Lilith killed Eve 1.0 after deciding the only man for her was already in Hell."

"So she killed Eve to guarantee she'd be in Hell with the Devil."

"Apparently, a group of angels had told her about how the Devil had been God's favorite. She had rejected Adam because she wanted the best. She interpreted God's ex-favorite angel-turned-Devil to be the best." Jordan glowered out at the streets around us. "She got what she wanted. A powerful woman became a powerful demon, and she got her son. Last time I had a chat with her, she bragged about winning the bet in creating a line stronger than Adam ever could. Compare Mammon to Cain or Abel, and Mammon wins hands down in every category she believes matters."

"Wow."

We continued to walk on through the city, and I realized I

hadn't been looking at the world the way I should have. There were demons everywhere. Demons sat in the shadows with twinkling eyes as they faded out of sight as the shadows shrunk. Tiny beetles, ash of a fallen angel, trickled down the drains as their wings clenched tightly shut. Despite this mass exodus back to Hell, there were some who remained. A man leaned out of the window of a car. A cruel smile played about his face as the smoke curled up from the cigarette clenched between his teeth. In the front seat was a man with runes tattooed around his throat. He was frowning and glancing in his rearview mirror. There was a motorcycle behind the car; the rider wore dark jeans and a brown leather jacket. Across his back was a hockey stick which I was quite certain wasn't just for hockey. I saw tiny sparks flying from the blade. The decal on the motorcycle's body was a silver eye which almost seemed alive. The dark visor of the helmet turned, and I could feel the eyes fall upon me.

Jordan glanced over his shoulder at me. "He would be a member of the Sons hunting the rune user."

"You've got to be kidding me. How many rogue magic users are there?" I grumbled leaning toward the curb to watch them down the street.

Jordan pulled me back, and we kept walking. "They're just passing through. Think—there's not even four hundred magic users. Why the heck would there be a good number going bad? We're a dying species. Some people are just jumping from the sinking ship a little too early."

Walking the city on foot was not my ideal Sunday evening. It was made even worse when the sun headed downwards, and some demons started popping up a bit early and looking at us like we were the best steak they'd seen in years. Jordan redirected twice before swearing.

"What's going on?" I asked turning in a circle to observe the sheer number of demons crawling out of their hiding places with us on the menu. "Should they be a little—I don't know—less singularly focused?"

"We've got a bit of a problem. When's April vacation for you?" Jordan asked, and I concentrated on him in confusion.

"Next week, why?"

"You're going to miss class tomorrow," he said and whistled. A motorcycle flew down the street without a rider.

"It just drove itself. I'm not getting on it." I gestured at the bike as it spun to a halt in front of us and burped up a helmet. Jordan slammed it into my chest.

"Get on the bike," he ordered.

There were not enough swearwords in the English language to cover how utterly screwed we were. It was evening. The city had just begun those darker hours when the demons could go frolicking, and an entire army of them was coming at us. They didn't run or march or stay in any sort of reasonable fashion. They came as fast as they could, slamming through the normal humans to get to where we stood.

"How about you get on the bike, and I go home?" I offered, but he pulled me onto the bike.

Jordon retorted, "Yes, what a great idea! Lead them right to where you sleep and can't control the entrances or the number of shadows. You also have a lofted bed and a roommate, right?"

Suffice to say, I didn't need his sardonic reply to know it was a stupid idea. "Your suggestion?"

He handed me a small laser pointer and a bag of glow in the dark bouncy balls. He wasn't the best Yoda.

"Fire at will," he commanded and turned the bike around, and we sped off in the opposite direction.

The laser pointer in my hand was not nearly enough. Sure, it got some funny looks and slowed down a few of the minor elemental demons, but with the number coming after us, the few who died didn't do much. I emptied the bag too quickly. In my defense, opening plastic bags on a bike was hard. The balls bounced and rolled and took out a few dumb ones. Most just hoisted their voids over them.

Jordan took us down and out of the city heading toward the suburbs when we stopped midway and drove straight into an empty alley and turned around. The hoard came in from all sides and boom—a massive fiery explosion without any messy human casualties. He kept the entire alley on fire for a few minutes killing wave after wave. Then, all of a sudden, the fire died down and a small sound like wind chimes hung in the air.

"Smite me," Jordan whispered, and we were off again.

He didn't try to be smooth. I clung for my life as we went through the insane maze of Rochester until we reached the edge of Brighton. Stopping the bike, he pulled me off and ran dragging me behind.

"Get rid of the helmet!" he yelled, throwing the bike aside like there was no expense to it. There was no way he could actually afford to abandon all this stuff, but I ditched the helmet on command.

"What's going on?" He ran faster, so I ran faster. "What's chasing us?"

"Safe house." He turned and sprinted down a street. "Too many shadows on a bike. I can keep the smaller ones from emerging through them, but there's a bigger fish surfacing."

The chimes which I hadn't heard after the first time sounded again, and we turned down another street. We stopped before an old boarder's house on the farthest edge of the city right before Brighton. It was tall with three visible levels and wider from front to back than from side to side. The white paint was chipped, and the stairs leading up to it looked like they would break any moment. There was a shed to the left of the house in just as much disrepair as the house itself. The shed was on a lower level of lawn a couple stone steps down from the street. Oddly enough, the lawn was pristine. The stone wall lining the left side around the shed stood watch over a large garden. In the garden were more flowers than I had ever seen before in my life. Some were huge and bright while others were delicate in shape and shade. There was a large stone against the back right side of the house. Thick bushes and wildflowers covered the stone seeming almost as tall as the house itself. I shifted my weight from one foot to the other as Jordan simply stared at the house as if considering his options. Honestly, I just wanted to sleep.

"If whatever is after us means I have to run and not lead it back to campus, maybe we shouldn't be standing out of the house where we are supposed to be laying low for the night," I grumbled trying to sound close to diplomatic and failing.

"Right," Jordan muttered and pulled the key from beneath a ceramic frog. We entered, and Jordan sealed the door behind us with a chalk ward.

I sat in the first chair I found and sighed as I removed my shoes and let my bag drop to the floor beside me. A glance to the back of the door, and I saw black chalk marks covering it, figure eights and other runes. Jordan approved them with a glance. He walked out of the room and came back barely a minute later with a book in his hand.

I glanced at it quickly. "What's this?"

"The Void Hours," Jordan began softly, "are the times when demons can pass between without assistance. But if they don't go back by the end, their voids are dried up by the sun. From sunset to sunrise, changes daily. Which is why..." He held up a farmer's almanac as he sat in the chair placed in the gap between the door and the window. "You always carry one of these. There is no such thing as a safe night, and don't get too comfortable during the day either. Always be on guard."

"Sure thing, Churchill. So I suppose no magic users live in the arctic?" I asked jokingly, but he frowned.

"Some do, but they're mostly those who believe the First Spell is a sin in and of itself," he explained as he gave me the book. "Never lose it. It will last ten years, but get the next one at least a year in advance. Don't take risks."

I nodded and reached around to grab my bag. Stuffing it in the biggest part, I looked up at him, expecting him to have already lost interest in teaching me, but he looked at me calmly. Something was off. He was still. Not epic hero-poses-for-camera cool guy still—the sort of statue-foreboding still. Sighing, he stood and gestured for me to follow. Moving through the halls of the three floor border house, I felt the history lingering in each creaking board. So many people had lived here. The house resonated with the souls who had entered and left within its walls. I idly wondered why Jordan seemed so uncertain of the old dwelling, but the thousand doors and small, self-contained rooms with a thousand shadowy nooks seemed the rational answer.

Jordan stopped by the edge of the stairs and pointed up. Leaning, I looked up; my heart dropped into my stomach.

Sitting on the edge of the stairs was the fattest blob of a creature I had ever seen. It was no more than two feet tall and weighed at least two hundred pounds. Its body was a large round ball with odd, salmon-colored tiny limbs and a round pin head. Its eyes were small and reminded me of a beetle. It sat not exactly on the stairs but over them on a cloud of rose-colored smoke. In its left hand was one of those long cigarettes the seductresses smoke in old shows. Every time it breathed out, the smoke formed the shape of a face moving in slow motion. It was an odd dark green color reminding me of decay, but the face was youthful and impatient looking. Wide eyes and pouting lips gave the face an even younger appearance. I had no idea which type it was, but it was definitely a demon.

Jordan stepped around me and into the full view of the demon. "How did you get into the house?"

It stuck out its bottom lip, which was black on the inside, and huffed. "Why would I need to get in?"

"When did you come here?" Jordan asked.

"When wasn't I here?" the demon retorted with a sneer.

"What reason is there for us to continue this?" Jordan smirked up at the fat blob which bounced down the stairs on its void, leaving the last puff of smoke up at the top to look down at us.

"With our kind, how could we ever stop?" the creature inquired, and its eyes flickered between Jordan and I, but I was smart enough not to say anything.

Jordan leaned forward, and the creature bounced down just one more step, so they were at eye level with each other. Jordan smiled as the demon glowered furiously at him, as if it were daring him to ask another question. Jordan's smirk grew as he asked, "Were you saying you're weak?"

"No, I'm saying you're an idiot," the demon hissed back and then clasped its pudgy hands over its mouth before letting them drop and glowering at Jordan. "You brutes are always so annoying!"

"And you Iggits are always so predictable."

Mentally, I made a note about the name, and the question game seemed to be an important part of being around them.

"What do you want, magic user?" The creature took a deep breath of the smoke. Suddenly, the face was beside it on the lower stair.

"How long have you been in this house?" Jordan asked, and it breathed out letting the face change into a frown.

"Three years. Thought it would be good to keep around it. Some idiots don't sense me and sleep without properly checking, so I get a quick meal."

"No wonder you've shrunk so much. Three years... two feet... you were eight feet tall. If you don't work a bit for your meals, you'll shrink into nothing," Jordan told it. The demon huffed and stretched itself. Where the fat blob had been, a tall thin humanoid stood with its arms crossed and a gray tailcoat with gray slacks.

"Just because I slouch at times doesn't mean I can't become tall enough to destroy your worthless human hide," it hissed. "Fear me yet, mortal?"

Jordan stuffed his hands in his pockets and rocked back on his heels. "You're only seven feet ten inches."

It rolled its eyes and looked at itself in the mirror across the hall and then panicked. Shoving me out of the way, it looked into the mirror. "I lost two inches. I lost two inches."

While the demon freaked, Jordan took out a match and lit it. As the scratching noise rang out, the demon fell silent and tensed. Before it could attack, Jordan tossed the lit match where the blob had once sat and where the face waited. The face twisted with fear, and the void evaporated as the man twisted and imploded while Jordan laughed.

"A match? Why am I not surprised? Laser pointers, light up balls, rave glow-in-the-dark crap! What's next?" I scoffed, but Jordan simply ignored me. I suppose I should have been more grateful certain demons were easy to deal with; I certainly am now.

"Iggits are among the lowest form of demons. To most humans, they appear as shadows or shade specters. They are the truth behind ghosts. The void of the most powerful Iggit is no bigger than a penny," he informed me, his thumb and forefinger shaped to demonstrate the size. "Fire and light dissolve voids as a void is created by distance and darkness. Fire and light illuminate and consume the void from within. The bigger the void, the bigger the flame or light must be. This is why only the most powerful of demons walks beneath the sun for more than a moment."

"Yeah, I got the idea from everything we'd done up until now. You are the worst teacher in the history of teachers." I huffed. He shrugged like my magic education wasn't on the line. "Work with me here, Obi-Wan!"

"Seriously? Did you just demote me?"

Ignoring his question, I pushed forward, "Isn't Hell a fiery pit of doom?"

"Ever read *Dante's Inferno?*" he asked.

"Nah, I've heard of it though. Popes in Hell and stuff." I shrugged. "It just seemed awfully long."

"Hell is made of absence. In a manner, it is a giant void. No light, no dark. No cold or warm. Absolute nothingness. If a human went there, they wouldn't even be able to perceive it. On the other hand, to magic users and demons, it can be felt. The closest feeling is of being cold, so a frozen hell is closer to the real deal than a flame-filled one."

"Okay, so light and fire." I nodded.

Jordan's tawny eyes narrowed. "You know what, if you want Yoda, you've got him. Classification systems—"

"Wait, no—I didn't mean—"

"Magic users classify demons by four things: size of the average void of the species, specie's specific abilities, method of removal, and nobility." He sat down on the stairs. "Most demons are straight forward. They want to kill you, and they have certain powers. Most are due to the manner of fracturing. Sometimes internal characteristics remain."

"What, like remnants of the angel?"

"Yes, now shut up. Iggits aren't nobility, but they are among a select few with a strange sort of carry over. Certain demons play

mind games. Others, like Iggits have to. Questions—you win, they
can't attack and answer all other questions honestly. Aim for the
pride. They also always slouch over their void. Get them to stand.
Again—pride," he instructed.

I studied the smudge where the Iggit had been. "But why?"

"Maybe they know they shouldn't eat souls. Maybe they
want to die like some Eashians but can't manage outright
suicide." Jordan raised an eyebrow. It took me longer than I'd
care to admit to realize I was supposed to be taking notes. I
grabbed my notebook from my bag and quickly tried to record
everything he'd said. Yoda parts not included.

"I get the Devil is king or whatever. Nobility, right? So Lilith
and Mammon too?" I asked.

"And Beelzebub," he replied.

"Is the Bible true on the Lucifer leading a rebellion thing?
And how does Beelzebub weigh in on things? Beelzebub is just
another name for the Lucifer in the Bible." I tried to rationalize
it in my head. "Are they co-conspirators or something?"

"Lucifer led the revolt, just like it says. However, Beelzebub
is a different angel who just followed suit," Jordan explained
lightly as if he was trying to keep from going into great detail.
"But honestly, I wasn't there. I only have second hand information about the formative events."

I tried to absorb all the information before quickly adding
the last bit into my notes. It just seemed insane how easily Jordan
talked about the mannerisms of Hell and the general workings of
it as well. I mean, seriously, who would have guessed the Devil
would have allowed his lady to go around with another dude
whose name sounds like a type of insect. He was the lord of the
flies and all. She even had Orpheus with Beelzebub.

"Why do demons tempt humans?" I asked.

"Demons don't tempt humans; they tempt magical humans.
Any other human is the Devil's property. Magical humans are
wild cards. Demons tempt magical humans because they want to
expand their voids. The bigger the void, the longer they can stay
on Earth, and believe me, not even demons want to be in Hell."

"Could a lower demon become an upper class demon by

getting enough souls? And why does a soul expand a void? Are souls like demon voids? But then why can we walk under the sun if they can't? Is it because ours are internal?" I rambled and then quickly stopped talking when I noticed the amused glance he sent my way.

"Demons are ranked because they fail to move up or down. A powerful demon will be powerful and gain enough souls to keep its void in a certain range. A lower class demon would fail and most likely attempt to consume a pure soul and end up killing itself. A human soul, when the human is good, is like a star. Radiant and warm, full of light and compassion. When it is dark, it is like a void. A spiraling black hole is never full enough, never sated, never at peace. An evil soul wants without end. A good soul wants in moderation—needs in moderation. Demons want to tempt souls into becoming as dark as possible in order to gain the most amount of void from the dead human." He leaned back in the chair and shot me a look telling me to continue.

My pen ran across the page as I tried to write all he had said. When I was done, I checked over my notes before asking, "You said souls could destroy demons with faith... what about atheists? Back during the viewing, you talked about kids believing in their parents, but what about atheists? They don't have faith like other people do."

Jordan gave me an odd look. "Faith is belief. You don't have to believe in something religious. Just like kids believe in their parents or even Santa, atheists believe in items beyond the religious."

"Santa? You're kidding." He remained serious, so I pushed on. "So—you believe Santa's going to save you, and poof—demon gone?"

"No, the soul shines then poof. Concentration on a source of positive belief—positive, morally good belief enables the soul to shine. The light produced by a human soul is brighter to a demon than any other light. When a baby is born, they're so small, but they just sort of believe in their parents. Think of the Christening. The hope and belief was so bright it attracted an angel. Babies believe those two people will protect them from the cold, the hunger, and the monsters. It takes an awful lot to make it go away." Jordan forced a small smile, not looking at me. "Some never stop. George didn't. When he does a risky job, he just thinks about his dad and bam—nothing can touch him." As if lost in his thoughts, Jordan pulled his wallet out and flipped a panel to look at a small picture. He caressed it with his thumb. "When you are ready, I'll teach you to look into a soul. It is the most beautiful and terrifying sight you could ever imagine."

I craned my neck and shuffled a bit only to catch a slim glance of a small baby picture before he slammed the leather wallet shut. He glowered at me, and I smiled innocently though I'm sure my guilt was clear to him. "Who's it a picture of?" I asked, giving up on the failed ruse of ingenuousness.

Jordan frowned and glanced down at the wallet before slipping it into an inside pocket in his leather jacket. "It was my son."

The stress he placed on the past tense shut me up rather swiftly. I stuttered a bit for something to say but could only flounder and mutter a small, "I'm sorry."

"Don't be," Jordan mumbled, exhaustion filling his voice. "He's better off never knowing who I am."

"So, he's alive?" The question left my lips before I realized how rude it was. "I'm sorry! I didn't mean, I mean, I..."

"His mother and I agreed he'd be safer if she raised him. My line of work is dangerous, and he..." He smiled wistfully. "I could barely believe he was mine. He had this soul, and it was just... devoid of the sin of my family."

"He's normal then?" I wondered aloud. "Did she not have magic like my mom?"

"Yeah." He frowned solemnly, and I knew I wasn't going to get anything else.

"What sin?"

Jordan sighed. "We talked about this, kid."

"The Covenant?" I offered, and he nodded. "She's got to have a name—same with the guy who delivered the message of salvation. Who was she?"

"She was the Witch of Endor, and he was the prophet Samuel," Jordan explained.

"The rogues we're hunting. They're from her line too, aren't they?" I waited until he nodded to continue. "So there are a good amount of evil magic users left?"

"Yes... but only a few, and they are being hunted by the Daughters of Tinashe. The rest of us hunt demons or hide, pretending the Covenant was never made. The Sons of Snorri work with unusual cases—rune users who don't otherwise have magic are considered mortals, so the Sons deal with them," Jordan explained. "You can't keep magic, ignore the Covenant, and still be good. Magic has a will of its own. When it can, it will help the demons get to you."

I thought over what he said, trying to absorb the information even as my brain yelled for sleep. "Just a couple more questions," I promised because I was sure he was just as tired. "If there are two groups dedicated to hunting rogues, why are we hunting the group in Rochester? And what was after us today?"

"I'm here on the behalf of the Daughters as a favor." He sighed, rubbing his palms over his eyes. "The thing coming after us was a horde. The demons, for however long the rogues can contain them, are willing to do what they can for their deals. They sent every single one of them after us, and unfortunately, somebody big caught wind of the chase and decided to join in."

"So, you could have handled the hoard if somebody hadn't joined in?" I asked skeptically.

He looked at me like I'd grown a second head. "Of course."

"You said there was a way to strip magic..." I trailed off uncertainly.

"A ceremony strips magic from someone born with it. Those people have no covenant with Heaven or Hell and are as free as any other human," Jordan softly said. "In the beginning, a lot of people went the no-magic way. Some dislike the idea of being like the rest of humanity. The Daughters aren't killing good people. They kill those who are corrupting the world and empowering demons but remain in denial about it, and they always offer the removal of magic and the alteration of ways before death."

"I guess."

Jordan sighed. "Magic was never a right. It was always a damning gift. On the day before your first spell, you'll have to decide whether to swear an oath to fighting demons, to give up your magic, or to run for your life and be hunted."

"Yeah, I'm good with the not being hunted part." I finished my notes and tried to memorize all I had been told. "So—big G God? With death and the whole..." I waved my hands around. When he didn't respond, I tried to translate further. "Covenant with big G God—Devil is real. I could go to Hell. Hell is real. I guess, with seeing monsters, Hell seems normal. It's totally—I always thought—it's just—"

"A bit overwhelming?" he filled in for me.

"It just sounds so easy. Give up your magic, but every time I think about it—I think I don't want to be normal," I admitted. I hoped I wouldn't be on trial years later with Jordan pointing to this moment before the Daughter cut off my head or something. "I'm not religious, Jordan. I don't go to church. I just want to know my dad. I want to be like him. But not—because he left, but I get why now considering..." I gestured at the windows and wards and where the Iggit had been.

"You don't have to be religious. This isn't about believing or not believing. This is about right and wrong. Demons are real. Demons are evil." He shrugged. "We kill them."

"So, God made the Covenant..." I was already down the rabbit hole of questionable topics. Might as well push it. "Christian God? Jewish Yahweh? Muslim Allah? Which one?"

"First, in Judaism, God is not called that." The coldness of his voice was penetrating and sent shivers up my spine. "Secondly, Allah is used by Arabic speakers in all three religions. Third, they are all the same being appealing to different groups through different manners. Fourth..." He stressed the word, and I felt like an ax was over my head and about to strike me dead. "My parents were on the hit list for the Daughters. My mother didn't believe in God. She believed in karma and ghosts to the point of paranoia, but never believed in demons. My father hunted demons down for revenge after my mother died, not for duty or the good of all humanity."

"So dad complexes run amok in the magical community," I mumbled, earning a glare.

Jordan frowned. "I've met the Devil, Jon, and I have to believe there's a bigger link in the food chain who could take him out at any moment."

"So what are you?" I knew it was a bad idea. Never talk about religion and politics. I just never learned.

"Religiously? I'm whatever will get me through the night." He stood and brushed off his pants though there was no dust. "Now, go to bed."

He walked away without another word toward a downstairs bedroom between the stairs and a sun porch. Turning away, I slowly walked alongside the stairs into another downstairs bedroom with two windows and a single door. I checked the windows and reinforced the infinity symbol on the back of the door before closing it and tossing my stuff beside the bed. There wasn't a closet in the room. I'm pretty sure it wasn't meant to be a bedroom, but the mounting stress kept me from complaining. Jumping onto the bed, I laid there staring up at the ceiling. I didn't even bother to get under the covers. I drifted off toward dream land and thought all well until a voice caught my ear.

"Jor-dan... Jor-dan." It was soft and almost would have passed unnoticed with the cover of a soft wind and a busy mind. There was no wind to shake the windows, but they shook anyways as a silver blur passed again and again. There was nothing but sleep to keep me and with the voice calling, I couldn't think of much else. "Jor-dan... Jor-dan." It was light and haunting. The voice sung in a child's octave. I braced myself on my arms and stared out the window at the foot of the bed as the silver blur swung across it and let it rattle. "Jor-dan... Jor-dan."

I stood and moved to look closer when Jordan's voice rang out from across the hall. "Sleep and leave the demon where it belongs."

I jumped and burrowed beneath the sheets, surrounded by the smell of dust and dead carnations. The demon circled, flying in looping circles. The windows shook and shimmered as small runes appeared around the frames. Whoever was calling for Jordan was no ordinary demon. It understood names, and Jordan had said only the top dogs of Hell understood the practice; those angels who landed and didn't shatter. Not to mention those demons who had never been angels at all. I had no desire to find out who was at the window. I covered my ears and fell into a deep sleep. Even in my dreams, the voice taunted me. Calling out Jordan's name as if it was a little child asking a friend to come out and play.

Twelve

Waking up in a strange house, I was on edge from the moment I stirred. I glanced down at my watch and groaned. It was officially the next day, if we have to count one in the morning as the next day. Today was Monday, and I hadn't contacted my mom. I opened up my cell phone to two missed calls and an angry text message. I sent her a quick text saying I was all right and spent far longer trying to decide what to tell her before just giving up and telling her I had come down with a bad virus and passed out. Slowly, I trudged to the sun porch.

"The voice last night..." I began and trailed off hoping he would get the idea, but he stayed silent as he moved around the large sun porch trying to rearrange the furniture. Looking at all the photographs, I knew for sure this was not his house. "Jordan, the demon... who was it? I mean, it had to be pretty powerful. It recognized your name. So—what was it?

"The demon isn't an 'it.' He is one of the few ones you can define as a 'he,'" he replied.

I swallowed even though my throat had dried up completely at his words. It was exactly what I had thought. "Who was he? One of the other two born demons? An upper class one?" I pressed, moving from the bench toward him. Frankly, the idea of having seen a second of those upper class, born demons was freaking me out. His amber eyes shifted between me and the doorway for a moment.

He faced me with this expression which told me I wouldn't

135

be able to handle the truth. In spite of it, he was going to tell me anyways. "The Devil has a name, Jon."

"The demon was..." I couldn't even manage to speak I was so horrified. I had heard the Devil.

"Yes... now let's get moving." He turned to walk back into the main area of the house when the light glimmering through the trees dimmed into shadows and the wind picked up. Sighing, he turned around. The swirling slowed, and a figure stared in through the window. Jordan scoffed and gestured to it. "Jon—meet the Devil."

The Devil looked like a little kid of no more than eight or nine with big violet eyes and oddly cropped silver hair. He was pale, and his grin seemed to take up the majority of his face. He seemed like an ordinary child though the hair and eyes were odd. Falling back into my seat, I was speechless. In a childish form, I would have thought the Devil would appear less frightening. It was all the more haunting to see great evil with a child's face. A familiar face. I just couldn't place where I'd seen it before.

Jordan sighed again and looked at the Devil with distain and a bit of boredom. I just stared straight at the ground thinking every prayer I could in my head over and over again. I didn't know many. I just knew the few I had picked up from television shows and books. I had never thought it possible for the Devil himself to get out of the underworld. It was hard enough fathoming demons were actually fallen angels and everything else Jordan said. To believe the Devil could just pop up to Earth whenever he felt like... It was too much.

"Jor-dan," the Devil called in his singsong voice. "Jor-dan."

Jordan rolled his eyes and removed his leather coat and set in on the back of his chair. I realized then we'd be staying longer than he had planned. I wanted to freak, but I didn't want Jordan to think I was a chicken or something, so I decided to play it cool. After the second hour of sitting in silence, I realized he had no intention of acknowledging my existence for the rest of the early morning. Sighing, I looked around for something to keep myself entertained, but found nothing but some dusty old books written so long ago no one cared to read them anymore. I picked up an atlas and almost laughed when I saw the Ottoman Empire written on one of the maps. I glanced up at Jordan almost hoping for a look of disgust at my antics, but he stared the Devil in the eye each time the fallen angel rounded the house and paused at the same window in the sun porch. He seemed absolutely consumed by the other's presence. His eyes were shadowed; the depth of his hatred was palpable in his dark glare.

"How long exactly can he stay around before he has to recharge his void?" I asked.

"The Devil has access to all dead non-magic souls turned to black holes in the history of humanity. How long do you think this might take?" Jordan sarcastically retorted. He took a deep breath. "This could well turn into a situation of what comes first: our starvation, his boredom, or Hell's need for order."

My eye fell to my hands, and I let out a pathetic, "Oh." And then it hit me. "Hell has order? Like a congress?"

Jordon snorted derisively. "Like a dictator."

I found myself nodding. It made sense after all. The kid was horrifying, and I could only image what he was like in his true dark celestial form. He was a fallen angel unlike all the rest, whole in body and mind. He was like a barely scratched car someone brought to a dump. Damaged in a manner which only made him immeasurably more terrifying for how little the damage changed the darkness of his heart. He was like one of those soldiers in movies about Spartans, Maasai, or the Roman Legion; the scars just made him much more dangerous. My eyes slipped closed, but I forced them open. I was scared to death to fall asleep again.

"How long are we going to try to stare down the Devil?" I asked, but Jordan ignored me. His eyes remained focused on the spot on the window pane. "I have to get back to the dorms."

"Not the best idea to walk past the Devil," he retorted.

I glanced between the windows and him. With no other options left, I embraced sleeping. I was exhausted and a screwed up sleep schedule could spell doom for tomorrow. Leaning against the wall, I fell asleep again pretty quickly. There was an odd lulling feeling to the silver swirl circling us. It was the Devil.

Recognizing the warmth filling me, I knew what dream I was being pulled into before I had fully shut my eyes. The dream wasn't actually a dream. It was a memory. Whenever I had been sad or lonely, there had been a memory waiting. I'd ended up napping a lot in fifth grade after we moved into our new apartment. I'd spent basically any night after a visit with my grandparents having this dream.

A tiny hand clinging to unimaginable warmth and being utterly safe was my first memory of him. I knew it was my dad holding my hand as I half-slept in my crib. I don't remember when this was, but I knew I was young in the dream. I clung so tightly to his hand, not wanting him to leave. My vision was blurry, and I wasn't fully able to wake up for some reason. Knowing now how my dad hunted demons, I'm sure this was actually before he was forced to leave on a hunt.

"Jonathan." His voice was low and poured over me like a warm breeze. "Hey, Jon." I'm pretty sure my dad was the first one to ever call me Jon. "I want you to know I love you. I'm so proud of you. I know you might not understand the decisions I've made, and I know your mother might never tell you all I want her to... but you have to understand I'm doing—I did do—the best I could. I'm not the father you deserve, Jon."

There was so much I wanted to say to him. I wanted to leap up years older than I was and never let go. He was my dad. I just wanted him. He didn't have to be perfect. I just needed him to be there. Even when my mom didn't talk about him, even when my grandparents insulted him—he was the strongest, bravest guy in the whole world. I used to think he was making promises. Then I grew up. He was leaving in this dream. Abandoning me because he thought he wasn't good enough. I was so angry at him for a while when I realized it. Now, with all the demons and the Devil, I understood. He was trying so hard to keep us safe, but there wasn't safe with magic.

"Jon..." he leaned forward over the rail of the cradle and kissed my forehead. "I want you to know I never wanted to leave you. If I had any choice in the matter, I'd be here for every second of your life." He chuckled—I'd like to think I got my laugh from him, low and rumbling, sort of like a storm in the old fashioned cliché way—he added, "Whether you liked it or not."

The hum of the ceiling fan droned out the following silence. Footsteps, shuffling down the hall to lean on the door, my mother looked in on my dad and me.

"You don't have to go." My mother's voice was gentle in the dream, pleading but gentle. "You could stay here... with us."

"You know I can't do so, Hannah." My father's voice left an impression so deep on my mind, I've always been certain it would have been visible from the moon. His voice was rough as if emotions had worn it thin.

"But you could!" The panic in my mother's voice rose. When I stirred, her voice became softer. "He's your son, and he needs his father. Whatever it is you're doing out there to protect those people, is it worth not being here to protect him?"

A rustling of fabric and the click of a small metal latch opening. "He'll be safe," he said, and the weight of the amulet around my neck for the first time followed.

"He's too young; he'll choke on it." My mother's hand brushed against me only to be gently pushed away.

"It's blessed; it can cause him no harm." I used to imagine my dad holding my mother's hands here or hugging her tightly. "Hannah, I got you both into this mess, and I won't let anything happen to either of you. Please, trust me."

"Don't go... please," she begged. "I love you."

"I love you too," my father told her. "Which is why I have to leave."

Then it happened. The hand to which I held so tightly pulled away. Baby version of me let out a shriek. I would like to think I knew he wasn't going to come back when I was actually living this memory. I know I was scared, but I also know babies get scared or cry for no reason whatsoever sometimes. In the dream, my eyes focused, and it was my mom who was looking down at me. Her face was stained with tears, and she hugged herself tightly.

She reached down and gently ran her fingers through my wispy hair. "It's okay, honey," she told me though I could tell she didn't believe it. "Daddy will come back and everything's going to be fine... I promise."

It was the only time she'd ever lied to me. I opened my eyes. My dream blurred as I traced along the edges of my mind. The first clear thought I had was Jordan was gone. Looking around, I noticed the Devil no longer swirled around the house. I jumped up and ran through the halls of the old house toward the side door. It was then I heard a noise from the kitchen. Turning, I slowly walked down the long, narrow hall ending in two doorways. To the right was a bathroom and to the left was the kitchen. I turned into the narrow doorway to see Jordan standing before the gas stove. He had a frying pan out, as well as a package of bacon. Toast, cut diagonally, was upon a plate in the middle of the long wooden table. A light blue towel was wrapped around the back of his neck catching the water dripping from his hair, so it wouldn't get onto his plain black T-shirt. His jacket was on the back of one of the chairs.

"Is he gone?" I asked looking toward the windows suspiciously, yet the silver blur never came, and the sounds of the morning were only of annoying birds and passing cars.

Jordan didn't answer at first, and I considered asking again but decided to just sit down. Grabbing a piece of toast, I tapped it against the table as I glanced around the 1920s style kitchen. The walls were covered in wallpaper of an unidentifiable variety, and the floors were tiles so old the grout seemed to be completely missing. The cabinets were attached to the wall shared with the hallway and were made of wood panels with countertop space built in to separate the top and bottom cabinets. Jordan turned from the stove and put the bacon on an empty plate placed at one of the seats. Jordan gave me a pointed glance, and I sat down. He tossed the pan into the sink and then pulled open the oven. The scent of cornbread filled with air as he placed it on the table.

"For now," Jordan said, and it took me a moment to connect he was answering my question.

If anyone else had done the whole affair of ignoring and then answering dramatically, it would have come across as stupid. With Jordan, it just felt ominous. I nibbled on the toast, more playing with it than eating it, while Jordan cut the cornbread and took about a third of the pieces. He ate quickly and ravenously unlike his usually meticulous mannerisms. Taking some bacon strips, I realized something had changed. It was subtle, a slight weariness to Jordan which hadn't been there the previous night. I blamed the fact his hair was no longer spiked and his piercings had been taken out. The silver earrings and eyebrow ring rested on a paper towel on the counter having recently been cleaned. I decided to blame the weariness on those tiny details as I wasn't exactly prepared to admit the growing possibility his weariness was connected to why the Devil was no longer outside.

"So, I've missed class, and I've got to deal with a missed call from my mom, so I think I'm heading back to campus now we're not getting chased by the big kahuna of the icy pits," I told him, and Jordan shrugged.

"We know they're somewhere in Brighton, so I'll zone in on the surrounding area and find their headquarters. When is your next free day?" he asked opening up a newspaper.

"I have two classes Tuesday and Thursday." I considered my week for a moment. "But my half-semester course ended last week, so I have this afternoon off as well as Wednesday afternoon, Friday afternoon, Saturday, and Sunday."

"Meet me at the shop at four o'clock in the afternoon on Friday. It should give me plenty of time to find where they are," Jordan replied. I went to open the door and Jordan stood. "Wait, let me warp fold you."

I groaned. "I can take a bus."

"This way you'll actually sound sick when you talk to your mother," he explained and pulled Lovejoy Hall into focus and sent me flying through without further warning. The hole closed behind me, and I stumbled into the building, reaching the bathroom in time before I vomited. From there, I went back to my room where Tyson was reading on his bed. He glanced up and then jumped up to help me to my bed.

"Dude, you look like crap!" he exclaimed. "Tell me you aren't trying drugs or something."

"Got stranded in Brighton," I explained. "Worst night ever."

He didn't seem convinced, but he let the subject drop, returning to his book with a simple, "Your notes from class are on the desk. I told the professor you had the flu and would e-mail."

I stumbled to my computer. "Thanks."

"No problem. Just... stop whatever this is before you get dragged in too deep," he warned.

Pressing send on the e-mail to my professors, I nodded and proceeded to pass out. I woke up around seven with a sticky note stuck to my face. Sitting up, I peeled the paper away and read it. It was from Tyson saying he had gone to dinner with Tommy, Joel, and Mike. On my desk beside my bed was a cup of instant noodles with another note; this one was from Tommy telling me to get better and offering help to deal with my current predicament. Needless to say, I'd have to deal with the offer another time. I grabbed my phone and dialed my home number hoping my mom wouldn't yell.

"Jon?" Her voice came over the line in a panic. "Are you okay? What happened last night? Don't give me any crap about being sick! I saw the picture of you in the jacket. What were you thinking?"

"I'm fine. I warded my dorm and everything. Jordan just wanted to make sure I was protected, considering the circumstances." Even as I said it, I knew I had screwed up.

"Circumstances? What circumstances are we talking about, Jonathan?" she pushed.

I knew I was already knee deep, so I decided to dig all the way down. "There's a rogue in Rochester—it's what Jordan is doing here. The rogue noticed I was his new apprentice and sent a small demon to scare me. The wards worked, and I'm fine, but Jordan got nervous."

"Of course, he did! A demon went after you!" She took a few deep breaths. "Jon, I know you don't remember, but—"

"Dad left because he thought he was endangering me," I interrupted, knowing where she was going. "I remember."

"You couldn't possibly remember. You weren't even two."

I sat up on the bed and looked around for the electric kettle Tyson kept hidden. "I don't know. I've dreamt about it a lot. I think training my magic has kind of gotten my head in order."

"But not in order enough to remember to call your mom who is worried sick after seeing you in a leather deathtrap!" she cried. "I get Jordan is trying to give you a piece of your dad. I knew you'd need training from someone eventually, but you don't have to do this. You could shut off the magic part of you forever. Jordan could take the magic away, and you could have a normal life—a better life than your father had."

"How can I know not having magic is better? There are no pictures of him in our house. You never talk about how you met or his family. I don't want to give up the one thing I have I know was his," I argued, finding the kettle under his bed. I debated a trip to the bathroom for water but ended up using the filtered water from Tyson's mini-fridge.

"All right then, let's talk about your father, and you can decide whether his life was a positive one," she retorted. "We met in a bar." I wasn't too surprised as I plugged in the kettle and waited for her to continue. "It started out as a one night stand then he tells me the next morning I'm pregnant." A little off where I thought we were going. "I thought he was crazy and ignored his contact information. He then levitated, and I was certain he was crazy. Two months later, I ran into him again. He had been hanging around the city to make sure I was fine. We went to the free clinic at my university, and there you were."

"Wow, I'm a one night stand baby. No wonder he wasn't keen on sticking around," I grumbled.

She scoffed, "Yes, you were. When I decided to keep you, he paid for an apartment and helped me. When my parents found out, he was there for me, so I asked about the levitating, and he went all out showing me trick after trick. At first, I had rational explanations, but I couldn't explain everything. Eventually, I had to admit magic was real. Things got worse when the Devil decided he wasn't happy your father was going to be a dad."

"He has reign over all corrupted mortal souls. Why didn't he just put something together and wipe me or you out," I asked.

"Your father covered the walls in wards, my car in wards, all my clothing had wards, and he spent months fighting back demon after demon sent our way. I almost gave up countless times. It's how his life was though. His mother—your grandmother—committed suicide. Your grandfather was an abusive monster, and your father never stopped believing he had forced me into a lose-lose position. He grew more certain he was destroying my life, and I fell more in love with him." Her voice grew brittle. I grabbed the kettle when it buzzed. "There was not a single day in his life where he was at peace, Jon. He never felt safe because he never was."

I poured the hot water over my noodles and said, "He was right though—in the end, the demons stopped when he left. I've had one threat since, and it was because some mage spotted me as the weak point for Jordan."

"You were the weak point for your father too, but the Devil still wanted you dead. The attacks might have stopped, and my life was a bit closer to normal than it had been in two years, but you're still his weak point, and if Jokul is still alive out there, the Devil will always want you dead whether your father is there or not," she replied.

"Well, good thing I haven't had a problem with the Devil," I lied.

My mom sighed over the line. "I can't lose you too, Jon. It terrifies me you keep going after this. Magic tortured your father. We both wanted so much more for you."

"Jordan has my back, and if things get too dangerous, I'll do it." I was pretty sure I was lying again. "I'll give the magic up. It's not like I'm going to leave school for this."

"You better not." She laughed, but it felt forced. "I love you, sweetie."

"Love you too, Mom."

"So, how's school besides missing a class today?"

"It's my first missed class," I defended, slurping up my noodles.

The rest of the conversation was mundane, but the relative normality of the jokes and topics were a welcome break from the last couple days.

Thirteen

I poked about the shop in the usual way. Seeing the Devil didn't have to change me, right? My life would be a hundred times easier if that were true. Instead, I dragged my fingers over books feeling for the discrepancies in depth against the shelves. Things weren't adding up. Or maybe they were, but not in a way I was particularly feeling great about. Jordan had a son. The guy was maybe mid-twenties, so having a kid wasn't that big of a deal. The real issue was Jordan had left his son. He had left his son like my dad had left me. His son's mother was mortal like mine was.

Jordan and George just kept on talking in their whispered-secret-friend-group way. They weren't the only ones in the shop. George had brought his children. The little girl, Sammy, was in her father's arms. Her forehead rested on her father's shoulder as she happily half-snored. Every once in a while, she'd jolt upright. Her gray eyes darted around to find her brother, who had recently turned four. The four-year-old was a menace. His name was R.J. though I had no idea what either initial represented. R. J. raced down one length of shelves then hid only to jump out and roar at me. Then off he went like a velociraptor with his elbows drawn to his chest and long jumping strides. Sammy thought it was great. After the fifth jump scare, I was ready to tape the kid to the ceiling.

"Rawr!" R.J. bellowed.

"Seriously!" I yelled back. His eyes widened. A heavy gaze fell onto my back. Whether it was Jordan or George didn't matter. My next move had to be made carefully. "Do you want to see what a real raptor looks like?"

He nodded so quickly I was sure his head was going to roll off. I twisted the air in the shop, and the modeling clay, which George had brought for R.J. to play with, glided into my hand. Squeezing the chunks together, I shaped it into a crude dinosaur. Practice made perfect, and this wasn't the first time I'd made a dinosaur. Picturing various museum displays from back home and from the Rochester Museum and Science Center, I sent a bolt of magic into the clay. A tiny velociraptor stood craning its head from side to side. R.J.'s jaw dropped.

"Can I hold it?" he asked.

I held out the dinosaur. "Be careful, okay? It's still clay."

He reached out, his little hands vibrating in barely contained excitement. Once he had the moving miniature dinosaur in his hands, he clapped both hands together, smashing the model to smithereens. The raptor twitched one last time, and the magic faded. R.J. shrieked with laughter then held out the smashed clay towards me.

"Again!" he cried.

Ten minutes later, Sammy had joined us on the floor and took turns with her elder brother smashing various magical clay creatures. As it was her turn, she requested I make an Amazonian princess. Smiling so hard her face was a bit red, she held the multicolored princess in her hands watching the model spin her lasso. R.J. waited patiently for all of thirty seconds before snatching the princess away and squishing her into the floor.

Sammy wailed, "No! Bad!"

Before anything could come of the two feuding siblings, George sauntered over and scooped the two up. "I think we're ready to go home and take our pre-dinner naps."

"Don't wanna nap," Sammy grumbled, but she was already slouching against her father's shoulder.

Turning to leave, George stared Jordan down. "This doesn't happen here. This doesn't happen in my city. This doesn't happen near my children."

"I'll do everything I can," Jordan replied, but George wasn't having it.

He marched up to Jordan with his children half-asleep in his arms. "We both know you aren't doing everything you can. I get you think it's a last resort, but if it comes to you doing what only you can do or letting them corrupt my city, make sure you can live with the consequences. Okay, Jordan? I'll get it if you can't do it, but you better be here for the fallout because I can't move my family again."

Jordan's lips set into a grim line. "I swear on the Covenant, George. One way or another, I will make this city safe for them."

George nodded curtly. "Work smarter."

"Not harder." Jordan opened the door, letting George disappear down the steps to a car parked right outside. He loaded the two kids in and drove off.

"So..." I dragged out the word waiting for some acknowledgement after Jordan closed the door. "Now that it's just the two of us. I sort of have some questions."

"Shoot."

"You have a son," I said, but before I could add the question part, Jordan interrupted me.

"No. Next question."

I sank back. "You left your kid. My dad left me. Is this a trend or something?"

"Safer to leave for everyone," Jordan replied.

Not what I wanted to hear. I wasn't sure what exactly I had wanted, but safety was an excuse to which I had previously been introduced. "Safer? Sure, safer even though I'm eighteen and have no idea what I'm doing. Super safe."

"If you don't like the answer, you can deal with it on your own time. Next question." Jordan cleared off the counter then flicked off the shop's lights. "Or are you ready to actually hunt now?"

"We have no idea where they are. Somewhere in Brighton isn't exactly a small range," I retorted. Running a hand through my hair, I organized my thoughts as we walked out the door. Jordan locked up behind us, and the ram's head was back out. I could have sworn the bratty thing was smirking. "Why do you have the Devil's attention? Why did my dad?"

"Too long a story. Next question."

Walking down the block beside him, I snorted. "Are you going to answer any of my questions?"

He smirked. "Of course."

"That one doesn't count." I pulled my beanie out of my pocket and stuck it on. "Where are we even going?"

"When rogues come around, they bring demons. Walking the streets and keeping them clean is the best we can do right now until we've narrowed down where they are," he said.

Heading up on Caroline Street, we were going a little too close to campus for my tastes when he turned towards Highland Park. I glanced at my phone. If I was lucky, nobody I knew would be there.

"I walk this way every time I go to the shop." The park drew closer, and I sent out a quick text to Tyson. "Why don't we head east? Maybe Winton or Buckland?"

"Giuseppe's Yeth are keeping other demons out of a large territory encompassing both. The most attractive place is going to be in one of the fields around the park," Jordan explained. The side of his lips twitched.

I resisted the urge to scowl when Tyson texted back: *walking to early dinner w/ Gma @ st john.* Sighing in relief, I tucked my phone back in my pocket. Grandma Scott would keep Tyson until almost dark, and Tyson would be heading down Highland Avenue. Luck was on my side for once.

"Okay. So the field near the outdoor stage or near the reservoir?" I asked picking up my pace. "The cemetery and the garden near the stone castle have more dark spaces where demons could hide a piece of their void, so they could easily move back and forth between there and Hell. We could go there instead."

Humming, Jordan glanced at me out of the corner of his eye. "Why would a cemetery not be the best place for demons?"

"Because ghosts like it too much?" I joked.

"Think, Jon."

"Strong emotions which ignite the soul burn away voids. People who visit graves or attend funerals would believe in an afterlife, so a cemetery gets cleared out with every funeral?" I posited, but the answer didn't sit well with me. "Mt. Hope is huge. It's a necropolis. There is no way the number of funerals in a day clears out the whole area."

"Nearly four hundred thousand buried in the last hundred and eighty or so years comes to around five a day on average," Jordan replied. "Not to mention joggers, visitors, and the regular staff."

Crossing into the park, I considered the stone castle between the outdoor stage and Mt. Hope. I'd never gone in, but plenty of weddings seemed to be happening. If a funeral or five could clear out something the size of Mt. Hope on a daily basis, a sentiment attached to weddings or other such events could certainly do the same. Fields it was then. Still, as long as Tyson was at St. John's with Grandma Scott, there wasn't anything to worry about.

"If emotion is so powerful, why isn't everywhere cleared out? There's seven billion people. Sure, some empty spaces, and I guess emotion doesn't really carry over too far between walls or into other houses or out of buildings." I paused and sighed. "Clearing out Mt. Hope only goes until the borders of the grounds, doesn't it?"

"Yep."

"Of course. What about areas without clear boundaries? Does a soul have an average radius?" I summoned my shield and pushed it outwards, becoming the magic equivalent of the bubble boy.

Slowing to a halt, Jordan faced me. "When souls collapse and darken, they condense. Smaller space, higher density. With the average soul, it can expand rather far, but the further it expands, the thinner it becomes. It really depends on the will of the individual."

"And people who fully believe in something, like kids, can expand further, right?" When Jordan nodded, I continued. "If demons don't rely on the normal physics of Earth, what are they even made of?"

"Essence."

I snorted, rolling my eyes. "Yeah, but what is 'essence'?"

"No idea." He shrugged. "It's not like we have many people

going around experimenting on demons. The best we get are bestiaries discussing observable characteristics."

My eyes slid over Jordan to a figure that looked to be waving at us. In dark wash jeans and University of Rochester windbreaker, I had a sinking feeling I knew exactly who it was. However, we were far enough in the park that there wasn't much to hide behind. I turned my back to the person in hopes he would think he'd mistaken who I was.

"No magical scientists then?"

Jordan smirked and glanced over his shoulder. "A friend of yours?"

"Nah, probably just a classmate or something," I lied just as Tyson yelled my name. My shoulders fell. "My roommate—Tyson Scott."

His lips twitched, but he didn't say a thing. Instead, Jordan sidestepped to stand beside me facing Tyson. Whether I wanted to introduce the two or not, Tyson was on a collision course with the more mythical part of my life. I closed my eyes. There had to be something I could do. My brain, unfortunately, didn't work fast enough. It was already too late.

"Jon!" Tyson ran toward us. "Hey! Perfect timing!"

Struggling for words, I turned to look at Jordan, but the jerk had up and ditched me. He didn't even bother to warp or anything. His leather-jacketed back was twenty or so feet away and shrinking with each passing second. If nothing else, that saved me from awkward introductions, but it would only triple the number of questions Tyson would have. I really didn't need him to be even more concerned about me.

Grimacing, I forced a smile and shifted to face Tyson. "I was actually heading back to the dorm. As much as I love Grandma Scott, I'd hate to intrude."

Tyson wasn't having any of it. "Who was that? That the guy with the motorcycle? He took you to the rave, yeah?" He squinted into the distance after Jordan.

"Oh, him? Yeah, that's Jordan. Helped me get my part time job," I replied.

"Jordan, huh? Which bookstore is that again?" We both

knew I'd never told him. He continued without pausing for me
to answer. We both knew I wouldn't have anyways. "Weird that
he just up and left. Not that he isn't nice. I'm not saying that;
after all I don't know the guy." A pointed expression was thrown
my way.

"I sort of pissed him off," I excused. There was probably
something I'd done today which bothered Jordan, so it wasn't a
total lie.

Tyson stared at me for a moment as if considering whether
pushing me was worth it. Shaking his head, he sighed. "You
don't have to come, but I'm worried about you."

"I know. I do want you guys to meet eventually." Total lie.
Didn't want them anywhere near each other. "He's kind of
introverted."

"He runs you ragged in the store and drags you out late," he
said. "You've been acting weird since you two met."

I had two options: one, make up a complete lie that would
ultimately make Tyson more suspicious, or I could halfway own
up to some part of the Jordan strangeness. For almost anyone
else, I'd have done the first, but he wasn't just my roommate. For
over seventeen years, I hadn't had a best friend, and now that I
had one, I didn't want to screw it up even for magic.

"He knew my dad."

Tyson's eyes widened. "Oh."

The one non-word basically summed up everything I
thought about Jordan on a daily basis. Jordan knew so much, and
he wasn't even telling me half of the stuff I needed, let alone
anything I wanted to hear about my dad. Tyson had grown up in
a two parent household. He had siblings who looked up to him,
and his remaining grandparents loved him. From aunts to uncles
to second and third cousins, Tyson had relatives in spades. Back
in the fall, his whole family came out to every home game.
They'd had me over for Thanksgiving when my mom couldn't get
the time off work. There weren't many people who knew how
much not having that meant to me. I couldn't tell Tyson everything. This, however, I needed to share with someone.

"Man." He reached out then let his hands drop as if fighting his tactile nature in an effort to adhere to my no-hug preference. "Are you sure you're okay?"

"Not a hundred percent," I admitted. "But it's way closer than I've ever been. My dad was born in Iceland."

"Wow! That's awesome."

"My new leather jacket," I said playing with the edges of it. "It was his."

Tyson broke down and wrapped an arm around my shoulder, guiding me toward St. John's. "We are having dinner with the great Henrietta Scott, and then you're filling me in on everything."

Not everything, but more than before perhaps. "Sure. That sounds good."

He grinned from ear to ear, and if he was still worried for me, I could only hope he'd think my issues were from learning more about my dad than anything illegal. One problem solved. If my luck kept heading in the right direction, maybe I'd even get a straight answer from Jordan someday.

Fourteen

Friday evening Jordan took me out to Brighton. He had an older-looking Honda motorcycle and helmets covered in runes. We ended up at this large weed-filled lot with a tiny house. It looked an awful lot like a bunker. There were huge patches of dirt surrounded by overgrown grass and a random tire. Considering the nice houses surrounding it, I wasn't shocked there were eviction notices and other notes on the iron, chain-linked fence surrounding the area.

"Blake is definitely in there." Jordan studied the house leaning against his parked motorcycle. "I go up and blow open the place. Demons go flying; you stay here and knock down whatever comes your way."

"Or I could go in with you," I offered.

"I'm going to kill him," Jordan informed me with a grim expression. "The job was to prevent this mess from spiraling out. The best idea is to make a point out of one of them."

"Why aren't we making a point out of Giuseppe?"

"He's with Rio and Madrid. One against three isn't the best," he explained.

I offered once more, "I could help."

Jordan rolled his eyes. "Stay put."

"Are we part of the mob? Is this a hit?" I called after him.

Jordan sauntered away, and a section of the fence melted as he crossed the road. He stepped through the gap and approached the door. I leaned against a nearby light pole watching Jordan approach the solid metal front door. The windows were boarded, and I was more than positive things were going to turn interesting rather quickly.

"Jon." I turned at the sound of my name. Tommy stood there in all his towering glory in a bright, neon-green shirt covered in purple and pink flowers. While the giant lineman was more Tyson's friend from the football team than mine, I couldn't avoid the mellow Puerto Rican.

"Oh, hey, Tommy."

He smiled, and his whole face looked like it was melting. "How're you feeling?"

"I'm fine." I stood up and tried to keep at least one eye on Jordan as he rapped his knuckles on the door like Blake would just answer.

"I know things have been heavy for you lately. Tyson's worried," Tommy noted. "He thinks you've been dragged into drugs or something."

"No drugs." I crossed my heart. "Just some late nights."

Tommy nodded; his lower lip pushed out a bit. I couldn't tell if he believed me or not until he said, "I know. Sometimes stuff gets too heavy, and you make yourself sick with nerves. My littlest sister has terrible anxiety."

I didn't know when he had gotten in front of me, but I kept trying to lean enough to watch Jordan who had both hands on the door and seemed to be concentrating on something or other. I could see waves of aura going up around him. Tommy was heading somewhere with this conversation, or at least, I hoped he was.

"It's too bad about your sister."

"Yeah." He shifted to the right, blocking my view. "Sometimes it's nice to know someone is there. It's okay, you know. She knew it was okay for her." Crap, we were headed to something strange here. "But sometimes, you got to know it's okay all around."

"Tommy..." I didn't even know what to say.

Tommy nodded. "It's cool, you know. You're having a hard time, but things get better. My sister's happy now with her girlfriend. It made her more relaxed in herself when she could tell us."

"Where are we headed here, Tommy?" I asked the question, but the destination was already pretty clear.

"The guys would be cool with it. You're a nice guy, Jon. It's okay if you're gay." He looked behind me at Jordan. "You're boyfriend's a little odd though."

"I'm not —" Jordan blew the door straight through the house. A loud shout told me all I needed to know Blake had been right on the other side.

Demons scattered from within the house having seemingly no recognition it was still late afternoon. Tommy spun around at the explosion but didn't seem to notice any of the demons. A group of Dorota headed our way with their trench coats wrapped tightly around them and sunglasses over their eyes. One reached forward to grab at me, but Tommy pushed me behind him and punched the demon in the face. While I was certain Tommy thought the demon would go flat on its back or cringe like a normal human, he didn't get what he thought. The Dorota's two mouths opened, and the glasses flew, revealing all four eyes glowing red as it stretched like something out of *The Matrix*. Before the Dorota could respond, I flicked the lighter and threw fire down on its void.

"What was that?" Tommy jumped back, and I turned the fire around on the rest of the Dorota. Some were smart enough to flee; others were not.

"Yeah, not gay; the guy's my magic mentor," I called over the roar of the fire.

Tommy moved, so his back was aligned to mine. "Magic?"

I grinned. "Magic, not gay, but yeah, definitely stressful."

"Oh." Tommy nodded and punched another Dorota. "It's cool."

I laughed, letting the fire fade. "Thanks."

"So..." He gestured at the house. "Magic mentor?"

"He's teaching me magic," I confirmed.

Tommy nodded and grabbed hold of a Dorota, throwing it over his head and across the street. The Dorota didn't even reach the ground when Jordan threw an LED disk straight into its void. His jacket was singed about the edge, but Jordan was otherwise fine.

"This your friend?" He gestured at Tommy. I nodded. "I like him. Punches demons."

Tommy's posture immediately became abashed. "Pleasure to meet you, sir. Thomas Hernandez-Washington."

Jordan reached forward and grabbed Tommy's hand, shaking it. "Call me Jordan."

"So, you're teaching Jon magic?" Tommy shifted from one foot to the next staring at the ground rather than Jordan.

"I am."

"And those were monsters?"

Jordan nodded. "Demons, Thomas; those were demons."

Tommy stared as if slowly processing everything before looking over at me. "I think this one's more stressful."

"Wouldn't know," I said.

Tommy assured, "Believe me; this one's more stressful."

Jordan glanced between us before shaking his head. "I don't want to know."

"I'd like to know what happened to Blake," I commented as Jordan pulled out his phone.

"Me too," Jordan replied.

Tommy watched us carefully. "Blake? Is he another demon?"

"We hunt demons; he summons demons," Jordan summed up. His attention then turned to his phone. "George? They've got a fifth."

"What?" Tommy and I said in unison for obviously different reasons.

"Fifth—they need a fifth to summon a powerful demon. This is bad," I informed Tommy. "Jordan—I'm assuming Blake got away. How?"

Jordan frowned but focused on me. "He had help. A wizard warped him out through a void."

"A—" I gaped. My mind raced to put two and two together. "Oh no—come on, Jordan. Warping is through Hell, isn't it?"

"Through Hell?" Tommy backed away. "I don't want to know. Explain it later."

"I can't believe you never told me I was vomiting after going through Hell!" I raged.

Jordan turned around, so his back was facing us. "Deacon Sullivan—well, of course I know now. He was the only one warping on this continent at this time. I know he said he had changed course at your request, but sometimes people lie." He paused, and I could hear George screaming something over the phone. "I don't know why they picked your city, George. Maybe it's personal."

The click ending call was so loud the supreme level of pissed off George had reached could be felt by all. Jordan stuffed his phone in his pocket and rubbed the back of his head.

"Jon?" Jordan said.

"I'm not getting a ride back, am I?" I asked, and he sighed.

Tommy glanced between us. "My car's back at the gym." He gestured to the huge gym facility a few blocks away.

"How did you even see me?"

"Grabbing late lunch." Tommy gestured at a small Italian restaurant a few places down on the side of the street we parked on. "I got to work a couple more hours, but it's fine if you want to hang out."

"It'd be awesome."

Jordan shoved the helmet I had been using into my arms. "Take care of it. Thank you very much, Thomas." He shook Tommy's hand again. "Hope you'll stick around and keep being an excellent friend. Sophomore? Junior?"

"Sophomore, sir," Tommy confirmed.

The corners of Jordan's lips twitched slightly upwards. "Fantastic," he said and off he went down the road. I could only guess he was going to meet with George to figure out where the summoning would be.

"Thanks for this, Tommy. I'm glad you were here." I patted Tommy on the back.

Tommy beamed brightly. "Magic's real. It's pretty cool."

"How long have you been working at the gym?" I asked.

"My dad owns one back home, so he knew the guy who had opened one of the franchises here. It was nice to have a familiar place to go to." Tommy shrugged.

We walked for a moment in silence, and then I said, "Um, people don't know about demon hunters."

"I won't tell anybody." Tommy glanced over at me. "I get how this sort of thing is."

"Now I just need to figure out how to convince Tyson I'm not on drugs while still doing my apprenticeship. There've been a few close calls," I admitted.

Being able to talk about this with someone other than my mom or Jordan was amazing. They weren't someone with whom I could call up and talk to about balancing demons and school-work. Tommy had always been a great friend, but he was the sort of guy who had a ton of friends and did his best to split his attention between his fraternity brothers, the footballers, and the connective outer circles. I highly doubted Tommy was expecting to find out both demons and magic were real when he approached me, trying to make sure I knew I'd always be accepted.

"If you're ever worried or need to talk." He let the rest sort of speak for itself.

I smiled as we walked toward the gym. "Thanks, Tommy. That means a lot."

Tommy bowed his head. "It's cool."

Fifteen

There was undoubtedly an emotion of mythological proportions running through my veins when we finally stood outside the complex only a day after Blake's grand escape. Up there on some floor was the crew we had been tracking. We were preparing for the primary confrontation. Sure, we had dealt with some interesting characters sent from one side or the other, but this time, we would be facing the magic users in the flesh. There would be no more demon doppelgangers, and this time, there would be a fifth. A fifth called Deacon Sullivan who I knew nothing about besides what I could glean from Blake's escape. He was a wizard. He was a male, and I had nothing beyond those two tiny pieces of information and his name. There wasn't a doorman to this building, but there was an electronic lock. The door was once again metal—thank you paranoid bunker enthusiasts—and the walls were bricked. Though the windows weren't boarded, they were caged in with iron rods.

"Why do we need these?" I gestured to the small box of bouncy balls which flashed like an epileptic nightmare with bright multicolored lights

"Tools," Jordan said. "These work well against minor demons—like the laser pointers. Manipulate them with air, and it's the same idea as fire pulled from a manual source, but this..." He bounced one of the balls. "Lasts longer and takes less energy. Additionally, if you get it in a void, it keeps causing damage even if you just let it go."

"Great." I stared down at the box, uncertain if this was the best or worst idea I had ever heard.

Probably the worst—demons and bouncy balls of doom didn't sound like a legitimate thing. I shoved the entire container in my jacket pocket for later use. Jordan stuffed a few in his pockets then dumped the rest, putting hooks in them with his magic. He then stretched like he was getting ready for a boxing match. All jumping around and swinging arms as he approached the building.

"Door or wall," Jordan said though his eyes were tracing the rough sides of the building upwards toward the roof above the third floor and down again.

"They'd know either way, wouldn't they?" I asked, and when he nodded, I shrugged. "Harder to defend from the outside."

He smirked. "You get in the door. I'll climb."

"What? No way! Separating is a bad idea." I could hear my voice crack at the idea in a way it hadn't in over a year.

Jordan didn't even bother to pretend he was listening to what I had to say regarding the matter. He leapt up a full story and stuck to the wall like a spider. Add a latex costume, and we'd have another web-slinger running around New York State. I turned to the door. It was a thick metal piece, and I knew, rationally, I didn't have time to just stare at the security precautions, but time wasn't on my side, so I put my middle finger on the edge of the door above the lock and my palm underneath.

The last—and only—time I had seen this done magically ended with Jordan sending the door straight into Henry Blake while I was distracted by Tommy. If he hadn't vanished thanks to the Dorotas he had on retainer and Deacon Sullivan, we would only be dealing with three who couldn't get another to join their group considering what Jordan had wanted to do to Blake. I hoped I could have a little more finesse. I traced my finger in a curve around the locking mechanism and door handle. The soft click was a greater reward than I thought I deserved. That the responding explosion sent the door up and not into me was thanks only to my instinctive shield and Jordan's ability to do multiple activities at once. He pulled the door up and slammed it through a window where it was sent back out by a freaking Japanese-style tiger and two gothic style gargoyles.

"You knew it was a trap," I accused when Jordan did a horizontal back flip on the building, narrowly avoiding a slightly more intimidating than I could have imagined army of butterflies.

He didn't get a chance to answer. Now, Henry Blake was impressive. He threw around magic liked a rookie boxer throws punches—without holding anything back. Bolts of plasma zigzagged from the ends of his fingers like heat-locked missiles. They chased Jordan, who had somehow turned into an acrobat. In jeans, white tee, and leather jacket, I wouldn't have thought he'd have much flexibility. I would have been wrong. He twisted and flipped this way and that, avoiding each blow. With a twist of his hand, Jordan sent Blake sprawling back into the crumbling building. Swirling blue and white spirals of fire followed, setting the whole thing on fire. Blake's screams echoed. They shook the house, sending cracks crawling outwards from the hole in the wall down to the foundation. When the fire stopped, a storm of Baoht stretched out like a giant, black, buzzing hand after Jordan. Neither was holding back, but it was obvious Blake was outmatched. Unfortunately, he wasn't on his own.

Rio was covered in sweat when she stormed forth from the other side of the wall with Madrid right behind her. With chapped red skin, Rio appeared to have gotten too close to Jordan's flames. While she and her niece both vastly outclassed me in experience, they were my best chance at being useful. Despite her living tattoos, Rio was just a psychic, and Madrid was a warlock, so we were—in theory—on par. Neither had eyes on me. Rio's skin puffed and waved around her as her runic beasts prepared to join the fray. Her niece stood shaking from the tips of her toes to her rapidly paling face. I crept closer, hoping I'd have the element of surprise on my side. Madrid's eyes whipped up to meet mine. Desperation radiated off her like a bad odor. Her nose crinkled as her lips twisted into a scowl. Before she could act, her aunt threw off her loose cardigan to reveal her bare arms.

"Self-righteous, little toad," Rio scoffed.

She whipped her head around wildly looking for Jordan, but what she got instead was me. The creatures on her arms struggled against the confines of her skin. In tight yoga pants and a shirt that was more front than back, she placed every bit of ink on display. If we hadn't been enemies, I'd think she was pretty wicked. A black widow spider crawled down her arm through a band of runes at her wrist. It went from two dimensions to three and leapt from her hands towards me. Actual size grew to Shelob proportions by the time the spider had landed.

"Stay out of the way, boy!" Rio shrieked.

Madrid sneered but said nothing. Her eyes shifted from me to search the field for Jordan who'd vanished, taking the Baoht with him. He was still around. I could feel him somewhere in the house, but I wasn't about to tell them that. Rio reached back to grab Madrid's hand. The stretching skin relaxed, and a stunned realization flooded me. Madrid was Rio's battery. With discipline to spare, Rio controlled the demons and runic beasts, but she was a psychic and could only power so much. Madrid was a warlock, and from the looks of it, one without much more discipline than I had. When Rio moved her attention mostly off me, I leapt. Thanks to Giuseppe, I understood why all those idiots in books with magic punch people rather than dealing with their problems via magic because in the heat of the moment, I completely forgot I had magic. There were only two absolutely crazy women who wanted my friend and me dead. Rio turned all her attention to me and sent every beast she had my way. Butterflies, gargoyles, spider, and tiger headed my way. The tiger's tail twitched back and forth as it stalked me, but a new rippling across Rio's back stole my attention. A gigantic Chinese dragon ripped its way through her skin, completely ignoring the rune pathway on Rio's wrist.

With a barrel roll, I tore Madrid further away and broke their contact. The dragon deflated like a balloon, leaving Rio's back covered in blood with strips of skin swinging behind her as she faced me. Madrid clawed at my face. Apparently, I wasn't the only one who had forgotten magic existed. She pulled back her hand, and a spiral of plasma collected in her palm before she sunk back to the ground motionless. The plasma dissipated when I stood, picking her up with me. Laying limp in my arms, I wasn't sure how to deal with Madrid having fainted mid-fight.

"Crap." I did my best to grab a better hold and not drop her. "You have got to be kidding me."

"Put her down, boy," Rio commanded as her butterflies fizzled against my shield.

The spider wobbled, losing a leg, then two before falling to the ground completely, sizzling into its miniature form. Soon, only a small speck of skin, blood, and ink sat in a dime-sized pool on the ground. Without her battery, Rio was in over her head. I couldn't let Madrid go, but I definitely didn't want to keep her this close if she suddenly woke up.

There was no pride in what I did next. Rio said to put Madrid down, so I did. The problem was I hadn't dropped my shield. I let Madrid go, and she hit my shield standing completely by leaning against the force of my magic. From the inside, I thought my shield was rather safe and warm. Apparently, to people who are not me, it was the equivalent of stabbing a generator with a metal rod. Madrid went down twitching like she was having a seizure. Knowing the shield would probably not feel great was on the far end of different from seeing it electrocute somebody. I pulled my shield inward from the bubble to Jordan's suggested bomb suit. The tiger sauntered closer, and I panicked pushing the shield out a little further from me. Again, not the best idea I've ever had. Madrid was now half in and half out, sizzling. Barbeque smell wafted through the shield as every bit of her that touched my magic was cooking. Rio shrieked and panicked, but her next move made things worse.

The tiger clawed at the shield, sizzling in its own right. Between attacking me and removing Madrid from my shield, the runic beast went about its business more like a demon. Powerful jaws grabbed ahold of Madrid' free arm which had fallen out of my shield. Madrid bolted upright screaming. The upward motion mixed with the tiger's pulling, wrenched her arm, but the big cat didn't stop there. It twisted its head, tugging Madrid harder. Her bones snapped. Skin tore, and her arm went more with the tiger.

Madrid screamed, "Stop! Make it stop!"

"I can't!" Rio shrieked, and the butterflies flew off in loops while the gargoyles sunk then smashed to the ground as solid stone. "Hold still. Just go limp!"

Blake and his Mugwærm flew from the house with Jordan hot on their heels. Giuseppe's Yeth howled, barreling down the streets. Their skeletal maws dripped acidic slobber which whittled through the pavement before they leapt into the fight with the rest of us. Hiding behind Giuseppe's horde, Blake was burnt with charred clothes and chunks of hair missing. His demonic doppelganger wasn't much better off.

Madrid screamed drawing Jordan's attention. He paused in his pursuit, but even as he turned to Rio, the earth shook and sharp spikes of stone rained down upon the Yeth. "Give up, Rio. If you want to save Madrid, you have to let the tiger go."

A white ball of flame hurtled at Jordan, but his shields held strong. The Yeth circled in a frenzy of gnashing jaws and terrible claws, and I was at its center. Demons of every shape and size scattered like bugs from beneath an overturned rock. With Rio's break in control, they attacked at random. Blake glanced back at us then vanished through a tear which closed too quickly for me to see his destination. Approaching Rio cautiously, Jordan held his palms towards her in a pacifying gesture. His eyes, however, flickered to me then to the tiger.

"Rio, for Madrid's sake, stop," Jordan said. Another fiery sphere crashed against his shield. Seeing his attacks weren't landing, Giuseppe turned his attention to me. The Yeth tightened in around me.

"Don't you see how cruel this world is?" Rio pleaded. "The people—the death—the destruction! Is this not Hell? You're meant to protect us."

"Well, the demons certainly give some credit to your point," Jordan acknowledged sending more of the balls out one by one. I had already given up and dumped all the little glowing suckers.

"Don't you dare mock me, boy! Our children flee from the south in droves. Mothers, fathers—whole families murdered in their sleep, and the Daughters do nothing but point fingers. How many of us have to die on your quest for penance?" She shrieked.

The horde of demons did their best to dodge the multi-colored balls glowing brighter with each bounce. Balls blasted light in all directions. While the hounds batted the plastic monstrosities away from each other and their voids, the rest didn't work so well together. I still had hooks in a few, but my aim wasn't great when I was caught between the tiger, Madrid passing out again, and more hellhounds than I'd care to think about. One drew too close to Madrid, and Rio sent the tiger off Madrid towards them. Giuseppe sucked air through his teeth in disappointment. The Yeth backed away, and the tiger returned before I could even feel a sense of relief that it had been gone.

Jordan sighed, running a hand through his hair. Glancing down at Madrid's bleeding form, he frowned. He wasn't the philosophical sort. Preferring demons to most people, Jordan would not be a Yoda with a catch phrase. There wouldn't be keen insight about light and dark existing in everyone. Most protagonists got wise mentors, but my mentor was nearly my age, and despite his wealth of knowledge, he wasn't the sort to dish out pearls of wisdom. He dealt better in pissing people off.

Jordan squared his shoulders, looked Rio straight in the eyes, and solemnly said, "Not in Nottingham."

Rio shrieked. Her magic flared around her in wild tangles. The tiger shifted its claws as it focused on Jordan, tearing its claws across Madrid's chest. "Madrid!" Rio rushed to her niece's side.

Resting his hands on his cane, Giuseppe lifted it into the air and slammed it down on the ground. The earth trembled. Rio's tiger melted as did the twisting remains of the rest of her runic beasts. With a desperate yank, Rio pulled Madrid free of my shield which I drew closer about me. Madrid leaned heavily on her aunt. Her left arm was a mangled mess of skin and broken bones. Blood rolled down her hand pouring down. I stepped back, trying to keep an eye on the demons surrounding me. There were too many, but I knew I had to try. Giuseppe's lips twitched, and the Yeth pawed the ground before vanishing through their voids in a great migration back to Hell. The smaller demons Rio and Madrid had indentured buzzed around having completely abandoned all pretense of being helpful.

"We have no time for such childishness," Giuseppe yelled. His eyes narrowed. "Deacon!"

The air behind the old mage shimmered. Like a tapestry being torn in two, the air split apart. In the growing gap, a brown field spread out. Henry Black stood in all his Civil War themed glory beside his demonic doppelganger. A step behind the two, there was another framed in shadows. I didn't get a good look at him, but I knew it had to be Deacon Sullivan. Giuseppe spun his cane and slammed it down again. The Yeth swarmed from the ground beneath mine and Jordan's feet. Fire and bouncing balls flew, but Rio managed to get herself and Madrid through the warp. With one last scowl, Giuseppe ducked through behind them.

With an animalistic roar, Jordan expanded his soul. White light mottled with three spots of black encompassed the yard. Illuminating light soon became blinding. I ducked my head clenching my eyes shut against the glow. Heat radiated. The Yeth howled in agony, twisting away but they had closed their ranks. Every attempt to sink back into Hell left their voids evaporated. Soon, only scattered remains stood between us and the void. Jordan swore, racing forward. His fingers scraped the lip of the warp, but it slammed tightly behind them before he could get hold. However, just before the warp snapped shut, I caught a single glimpse of a form in the distant corner of the field. Brown slats tethered together into a long house with a curled roof – a Seneca long house. There was only one in the whole of Rochester.

"Ganondagan," I whispered and ran to Jordan. "They're doing it at Ganondagan!"

"Where?" He pulled at the wisps of magic left in the air as he asked.

"It's a historic site," I explained. "There's sacred ground and burial sites on the land." I pulled my phone out to find a map only to have Jordan shove my hand aside.

"I have a read on them. They're using the burial wards to block me."

"You're a wizard!" I exclaimed. "How did Giuseppe get past you?"

Jordan grabbed the field near Ganondagan with his magic and tore the distance between where we stood and where we were headed apart. "Five against one, and I've got some scruples left."

The field spread out before us. Long grass curled brown with recently mowed green trailing through the field. Dragging me through, Jordan let the warp weave back together behind us. He ran past the long house as a storm gathered over head. I ran to keep up, but he seemed to be flying over the ground. Blue lightning grazed the tops of the trees. Dark clouds lumbered low enough I might have reached up and touched them.

I had read of Ganondagan in a packet talking about the diversity and history of Rochester before deciding to go to university in the area. The ominous feel didn't match the smiling children I remembered. Those kids had been having fun playing historic games while doing traditional crafts. Kids like R.J. and Sammy came here. If Jordan was right, and he often was, the summoning would leave catastrophic ripples in its wake. The whole of Rochester would be marked and practically radioactive.

We headed over a small rise in the field, and beyond a shallow tree line, the five rogues stood in a break before a sharp downhill drop. All hands were facing inward. Madrid was barely standing, and with a sharp breath, she collapsed into a crouch. I had thought Jordan would march straight on through and stop the summoning, but he stilled. His entire body tensed, and he exhaled harshly.

"Crap," he murmured. "George is going to be pissed."

None of the rogues noticed us on the opposite side of the thin line of trees. All eyes were staring at the air in front of them. There wasn't a pentagram carved into the ground. There weren't runes or any symbols I'd ever read about or seen in any movie. There were, however, six circles. Each rogue stood in one, and a larger circle was before them. Well, stood wasn't exactly correct. Giuseppe and Blake were fine. Rio stood though she leaned towards Madrid's circle. Madrid wavered in her crouch. Her functional hand was one fire, but no matter how she tried to cauterize her wounds, they just stretched wider and bled faster. Magic had a will of its own, and saving Madrid wasn't something it was interested in doing.

Deacon wobbled a bit. "Blake? You..." He blinked collapsing to his knees. "You liar. You said you had the soul."

He fell against the ground. His chest stilled. A growing cloud leaked up from the ground in the center circle. With a shriek, Madrid's fire died out. She wavered then hit the dirt. Blood pooled around her, but she struggled to push herself upright. We stayed still behind the trees. Jordan's lips moved. He mouthed numbers counting down, but I didn't know what he was counting toward. His promise to George had been to stop the summoning or deal with the consequences. The summoning had come and gone. Whatever the ramifications were, Jordan seemed to know to a count when they'd arrive.

"Heal her!" Rio demanded, ignoring her own bleeding back. "Mammon, I command—"

Madrid shook. Darkness slipped like smoke from the center circle into Madrid's. It curled around her. She lifted herself up, stretching out her newly healed arm. A smile broke across her face. Then said face smashed back down into the ground. Completely healed to the point where even her clothing was cleaned and sewn back together like it'd never been damaged, but still, Madrid was dead. Rio jumped from her circle running to her niece's side. She never made it. Two steps out of her circle, Rio joined Madrid on the ground. Blood spurted out her back as she convulsed. Flashing of ink shimmered over her skin.

Having stopped his silent count, Jordan stepped between the darkness and me. He gently pushed me behind him. With a finger to his lips, he stretched out a hand gesturing to the edges of the inner circle and back to the field. In pulsing waves, the emotions which had covered the field ebbed away. Joy of nature and attributions of history were wiped away beneath an unbearable weight of absence. The closest feeling I'd ever experienced to it was loneliness. The bitterness of winter melded with a sense of powerlessness. It was almost a physical blow knocking me backwards.

In his circle, Blake fidgeted like he could feel the weight too. His eyes stuck to the darkness. Paler and still charred from his fight with Jordan, Blake didn't appear as terrifying as the Mugwærm version of him had. He was just another magical human who screwed up. Jordan kept me behind him. Kept me waiting though I had no idea why missing the summoning kept us at a distance for so long. Sure, Mammon was dropping them like flies, but it didn't stop what was coming.

The storm inside the large circle swirled with a snort. "Three down—which of you will demand something next?"

"We command you do us no harm," Blake cried.

The dark cloud laughed. If I had any illusions about summoning putting the demon completely in the summoner's power, this would have put them to rest. We were just fleshy little jokes to Mammon. Singing softly to himself, the son of the Devil crooned, "Four little birds sitting in a tree, a cat ate one then there were three. Three little birds—what could I do?—another one died then there were two."

"You must obey our commands and do us no harm," Blake tried again to regain control.

Mammon solidified before them. He looked the same as before though there was a change around his eyes separating him further from the rest of humanity. While they'd been auburn before, his eyes were entirely red. There wasn't a single spot of white or black in them. Blake paled, and Giuseppe smirked like it was all just one great game he was winning. With a nod of his head, Jordan led me closer to the circle. We passed through the trees and kept low to the ground. Once again, Jordan started to silently count.

A gunshot sent the two of us sprawling to the ground. I'd heard gunshots before, but never so close up. My ears rang even as Giuseppe tucked the revolver back into the small of his back. Mammon laughed, and the thunder rolled overhead like God was laughing too. Blake clutched his chest, but he couldn't stop the bleeding any more than Madrid could have healed herself. He sank to the ground. Giuseppe didn't even bother waiting to make sure he died. The mage turned to Mammon with a cluck of his tongue.

"We have a job to do. The rules are rote," Giuseppe spoke slowly and with a sort of terrible determination like he was drawing to the end of an incredibly long race. For him, this moment had been years in the making. "Now..." He stepped out of his circle. "Come."

Giuseppe left, and Mammon swaggered behind him as if this was just another detour he couldn't wait to see the end of. I went to stand, but Jordan's hand landed on my back keeping me down. He shook his head pointing towards Blake's circle. Darkness shifted low to the ground. When Giuseppe had vanished out of view towards the nearest roadway, the low hanging darkness grew. Mammon formed beside Blake. His eyes slipped from red to human-like amber.

"Heal me," Blake commanded. He reached out a bloody hand grabbing at Mammon's shirt. "Do it."

Mammon plucked out the bullet, and the wound sealed. "The first."

"Bring me my wife," Blake commanded. "Pull her out of its void." He slammed his fist against the earth, and the Mugwærm appeared spinning the pocket watch around and around on its chain. The body of the demon was still Blake's, but the face was pure white with blue lips stretched in an overly large smile. The teeth weren't visible, yet they were a presence all their own waiting in the shadows.

Jordan pushed up. When I moved to follow, he shoved me back down and glared me into submission. Neither Mammon nor Blake noticed as Jordan headed towards them. Lightning struck around the circle, hitting the Mugwærm's void even as the demon tried to move out of Mammon's way. It failed and burned until it exploded in sparkling white powder.

"There's the second," Mammon said. Blake gaped. His face paled as he stood. His eyes fell onto Rio and Madrid.

"Heal them," Blake gestured at the two dead rogues. "You had your quarry of three."

Mammon's eyes narrowed. "Are you certain?"

"Yes, of course, I'm not as cruel as him," Blake gritted out.

"Fine." Mammon shrugged, and then both Rio and Madrid stirred. "I'm keeping what's mine."

"They're yours when they're dead," Blake retorted as he straightened to look Mammon in the eyes. His legs trembled beneath him despite his bravado.

Jordan was almost on top of them. Red bled out, covering Mammon's eyes once more. Without pupils, I could feel the weight of his gaze fall onto me then shift. He'd noticed even if Blake hadn't.

Mammon turned his attention back to Blake. He observed the man's tremors then raised his eyes to the other's face meeting Blake's gaze before smirking. "Soon."

Blake glared, but didn't argue the point. "Leave us to our own devices."

Mammon laughed. The shadow of his void loomed above us, and then Mammon was gone. Blake turned his back to us. With his pocket watch in hand, he ignored the world around him as Jordon stepped out beside the ring of circles near Deacon's corpse. Blake's shoulders fell, and his head bowed. I slowly moved to my feet. Jordan held out his hand. His back toward me, Jordan expanded out his soul. Blake didn't move.

Jordan glanced at me. "Duck, Jon."

I did as commanded without thinking, and a dark metal iron rod flew through the air into Jordan's outstretched hand. Even though I'd never seen it before, I knew what the rod was: a fire poker. The metal glowed white at the tip radiating waves of heat. Jordan glowed—his soul shifting outside the confines of his body to project a layer of armor over his skin. Thrusting the iron rod into the sky, Jordan reached forward toward Madrid and Rio who were slowly twitching back to life.

They moved like zombies. Each move they made was jerky and rough. Rio put her hands against the ground with a groan. She pushed upwards only to catch sight of Jordan. Her eyes widened, and she scuttled backwards but not quickly enough. Lightning struck the rod, and Jordan reached his free hand towards her. Plasma bolted from his fingers, but it twisted into tendrils and wound around her throat like rope. Rio dove for

Madrid's hand, but Jordan threw her backwards forming a crater in the ground. The psychic convulsed as her skin heated around the tendrils. He brought the iron rod down pierced through her chest. Rio shrieked and clawed. White light pressed against her skin as the runic beasts once had. Her eyes blazed then sunk down, scarred into husks as she stilled, then exploded like the Mugwærm had.

Madrid stood staring. When Jordan lifted the rod and turned towards her, she jolted, but she wasn't quick enough. I leapt to my feet running. Jordan drew back with the rod and sent it flying. It soared through the air and Madrid's chest to pin her into a tree. Lightning struck the old trunk once then twice then countless times in quick succession until there was nothing left of her.

All the while, Blake remained oblivious. Skidding to a stop next to Jordan, I realized why. Wisps of darkness formed a dome around the southern magic user. Mammon had effectively left him easy prey. Jordan sighed, glancing towards the empty circles then to the one where Deacon lay.

"Don't try that," Jordan said. He pointed towards the two's cinder remains. "When a soul is swallowed then brought back, the dark parts aren't exactly connected to like before. They're almost like a void for a very long time. Since they were fresh, I could emulate them like any other void."

My stomach sank. "I think I'm going to be sick."

At my words, the veil of darkness slithered away. Blake glanced over his shoulder slowly. When his eyes landed on us, they widened, and he scrambled to turn around to get away. The iron rod flew through the air. Jordan caught the poker. Hefting it above his head, he sent fire up his arm and down the iron. Screaming, Blake ran.

"We have to go after Giuseppe," I screamed though the world was deadly quiet.

Jordan remained silent. He brought the fire iron down and caught Blake's soul with the point of the curled secondary spike. Dragging Blake backwards across the graveyard, Jordan held the poker with one hand. A plasma tendril shot forward wrapping around Blake's neck. Clawing at his own throat, Blake struggled, sending earth and fire and lightning back at Jordan, but the wizard just kept pulling him in. Jordan drummed his fingers in the air, and the plasma faded. Catching his index on a graying swirl of multicolored light, Jordan tugged. The calico colors had me guessing until I realized what I was seeing. He'd taken hold of Blake's soul. The threads of Blake's soul crawled up Jordan's fingers as if desperate to flee from Blake.

"Help me!" Blake reached out to me, clawing at the dirt and pleading for his life, "I had no idea what would happen! It was Giuseppe! He lied to me! It was them! Please, stop! Help me! Boy! Boy—Jonathan!" I glanced up at my name. "Help me! Please stop him! I'm innocent! I can change! I haven't gone dark yet!"

Jordan asked, "What about Deacon?"

Blake's eyes were wide and flickering in his panic. "Who?"

"Deacon," Jordan said. "He was told Mammon could bring back his dead son. A two-year-old couldn't have been swallowed and couldn't have been brought back."

"Oh." He paled. "Deacon."

"Yes, Deacon." Jordan's eyes were overwhelmed by the bright white light of his soul then two black pits formed within the light, flickering false eyes. "Where was his help?" Jordan grabbed Blake chin forcing him to look at the glazed-eyed corpse of Deacon Sullivan.

"He knew the risk!"

Jordan laughed—low and dark and inhuman like thunder. "So did you," he intoned and slammed the rod through Blake's face. His skull crunched in upon itself. Blake stilled for a moment before his body convulsed and exploded like those before him had. Leaving the rod buried in the ground, Jordan inhaled slowly. With an exhale, he stepped back and clamped down the light of his soul, so I couldn't see its manifestation anymore.

"Doesn't it mean Mammon has his soul too? And what about Rio and Madrid? They die, reincarnate thanks to a demon, and die again. Where's the Winchesters?" I gestured at the bodies. "With just Giuseppe, doesn't this all mean he has almost his full payment?"

Jordan smirked. "Why do suspicious people pay half up

front and half when the job is done?"

"Because full payment would mean the other party could run off without completing the deal," I retorted, and the validity of what he said sank in. "But Mammon's still getting more souls for his void."

"No." Jordan gestured at the scorch marks around the summoning. "He's getting more than he was promised."

"So—he's already reached full payment. He has no reason to stick around."

"Unless he wants to make it a full five, but his count isn't the problem. With those demons dead and the extra souls going his way, he might not realize something else has snuck its way into his void." Jordan smirked before he drew the coin necklace from his pocket.

The bits of metal clinked together, casting neon blue sparks into the twilight of the setting sun. Holding up his opposite hand, he showed the strange blob of Blake's soul. Small objects flew from Jordan's pockets. Several firecrackers, sparklers, matches, flash bombs, and several other things I couldn't identify. They poured into Blake's soul. Some even interwove into the coin necklace. Pressing the coins to the soul, the light swallowed it along with everything else. Jordan peeled the soul from his arm and threw it into the air.

"Fly home!" he commanded.

The soul flew on a bolt of blue lightning across the grave-yard and into the night and the city beyond. When I finally drew my eyes from the sight, Jordan had waltzed into the center of the inner summoning circle where Mammon had previously stood. He threw his leather jacket at my face, which I fumblingly caught, before lifting his left foot and slamming it back down upon the ground. Blue sparks kicked up from the dust. The wind hissed a whistling breath. Thrusting his hands skyward, Jordan pulled down the sky. The dark clouds above our heads bent beneath Jordan's force. The smoke and ash at our feet trembled and drained toward the circle's center. He dragged the spot his fingers had hooked upon to the ground and held it there in a crouch. It was like watching Atlas drop the globe. Sweat glistened on his brow and blue sparks traced the ripples he had made. With a long breath, he released the section, and the tension snapped the bit back into place.

The rippling echoed outward and upwards, sending all sorts of creatures from their hiding places. Bugs crawled furiously away from the area as birds took to the sky. Pebbles on the ground shook then jumped in small bounces across the ground like a small earthquake was shaking western New York. Leaves rustled above head, and the loud buzzing, like a tuning fork, started as a whisper before increasing to a deafening ring. The area before Jordan became concave then collapsed in upon itself before exploding outwards in the form of a man. There was neither smoke nor the smell of brimstone. The air smelled like burnt sugar for a moment before curdling, ending on a pungent bitter smell of burnt coffee. When the air settled, Mammon stood before Jordan, swinging his necklace with a small smirk and narrowed eyes.

"Must we play this game, Jordan?" Mammon murmured before slowly leaning forward to stage whisper in Jordan's ear. "Four for five—one little uncapped pen from a flush."

Jordan rolled his shoulders and tilted his neck away, then looked back at Mammon to whisper to the demon in the same way, "Did your mother never teach you not to take candy from a stranger?"

Mammon's eyebrows knotted. "What?"

"I could lace it with anything," Jordan informed him and the space behind Mammon lit up. Every explosive Jordan had shoved into Blake's soul and stuck in the necklace sparked light and heat throughout the whole of Mammon's void.

In the oncoming night, I hadn't even realized Mammon had put his void back up around him. Light blared up from deep within with each new resounding explosion. Mammon faced his void. His face paled as he struggled to reach into the void, shifting it around his hands. There was no way he could find everything. He'd already melded Blake's soul into his void. It was now one of hundreds. Finding it was going to take more time than his void had. Additionally, as long as Mammon's void was under attack from within, he couldn't go through it back to Hell without putting his essence at risk. Jordan setting a trap in them hadn't even crossed his mind. Blue exploded into reds, whites, and greens better than any Fourth of July show.

Mammon gritted his teeth, glaring at Jordan. With each successive explosion, his shoulders tightened until he said, "When the Devil finally drags you down, I'm going to enjoy pulling your soul apart stitch by stitch."

"Funny, isn't it? Your daddy and I already agreed my first southbound fun time was going to be kicking your oedipal self back to the First Day. I'd say we'll see, but we both know who Lucy likes more." Jordan tilted his chin up and smirked.

"Unlike the others, he completed the deal, Jordan," Mammon replied. "He's got a tiny piece of void in a pen in his pocket, and we made a deal. I'm not ready to give up on the piece of void or the rest waiting in the meat suit."

Jordan shrugged. He tugged the fire poker free and spun the fire iron round before leaning on it like a cane. "I can pull those all out." Mammon's eyes narrowed to blood-red slits, and we all knew what Jordan was going to say. "Let's make a deal."

"I'd rather tear your intestines out through your throat." Mammon winced at a particularly nasty explosion in his void. The black wall crumbled in behind him. Countless centuries of work ruined in a few minutes.

"I think there is a glass of Greek fire in there somewhere." Jordan sighed dramatically, turning to look back at me. "Do you remember how I set it? I basically just summoned everything in the shop's backroom I thought would be useful. A few fireworks, some sparklers, LED gadgets, and—what was the last thing?"

"The shop..." Mammon backed up and started frantically manipulating his void once more. "You wouldn't dare."

"I think Morgan made it especially for you."

The well-groomed demon of the day was gone. In his place, a panicking version frantically tore through his void searching for whatever Jordan had thrown into the mix when he let those souls go. It was definitely a trick I wanted to learn. Mammon was impressive. He hadn't been the least bit afraid up until this point, just slowly getting more and more pissed off. Whatever this Morgan person had made was something Mammon had experienced before. Something Mammon never wanted to deal with again.

"Fine!" he cried. "Deal! I'll head back to Hell; deal's off with Giuseppe. He can keep his blasted soul."

"And you stay in Hell for ten Earth years." Jordan spun the iron rod on its tip like a top against the ground.

Mammon gaped. "What? It's too much."

I wasn't even sure Jordan could make that sort of deal, but I wasn't about to argue. The good guys were starting to win a few. If we were going to be keeping Jordan's promise to George, we had to pull out all the stops.

"If you swear it, I will make certain no demon gets his soul."

Mammon's eyes sparkled. "Oh." His smirk returned with all the same bravado. "Yes—that's perfect. I swear it on Hell, Heaven, Earth, and the Covenant."

Jordan didn't flinch, but I ducked behind him as everything he had put in the void flew out and detonated over the field. Mammon sunk back into smoke with a chuckle, crawling back through his void into Hell. Once he was gone, the clouds above us cleared. Endless stars sat in a dark blue sky above us, and silence reigned when the explosions ceased. The corruption, however, stuck like a vile stink over the field, spreading throughout. It wasn't exactly the apocalyptic scenario I'd been led to believe it would be.

"What now?" I asked, stepping forward to stand beside Jordan.

Jordan frowned and let the iron rod drop to the ground. "Now, we fulfill our bargain and make sure Giuseppe does not attempt this a second time."

"Warping?" I cringed as I asked. I had no desire to warp again.

My stomach was still rather queasy from the last journey. Knowing I had traveled through Hell to get here only tied my innards in tighter knots. None of this was going how I had expected. Demon hunting had been downright exhilarating until the horde, and the whole detective aspect had me intrigued even if Jordan hadn't let me in on most of it. The murder didn't. Jordan had killed three people without a second thought. I had to keep reminding myself they'd gone in knowing Deacon Sullivan was going to get killed. They'd summoned Mammon.

"No." Jordan turned and headed down the hill. "We have time."

"I thought the summoning was going to level the city?" I asked, avoiding looking at the piles of ash that had been people.

Jordan snorted. "Wait a few months."

"I don't get it. What's going to happen?" I pushed.

"It'll start with strange storms. Demons will get attracted to the area, and even bigger storms will follow. The beacon for demons has been lit. It will take years to put it out." He glanced over at me. "The area back there will be corrupted. It'll be like an easy access doorway. I'll have to come back and clean it out later. Probably scour the city for a horde or two."

I nodded, shoving my hands into my pockets. "George's going to be pissed."

"Yeah, well—if we'd let those three walk around, things would have been far worse," Jordan said.

Before I could ask exactly how much worse, a revving engine echoed up the road. The motorcycle rolled up toward us. When the machine had arrived, the kickstand dropped with a click before the engine clicked off with a purr. Small LED lights wove around the bike like bugs. They came across a few hooks, sizzling the demons' lines away before flying back into Jordan's pockets. Straddling the bike, Jordan reached up, catching his helmet which came flying up the road. I waited, expecting him to summon another, but he just glanced up at me.

"Jon, try calling the helmet."

I raised a hand, and nothing happened. "Do we really have time for this? What if it has demons in it?"

"Ignite your soul," he retorted like it was the easiest thing to do. His eyes were already ahead at wherever we were going.

"I haven't figured out how to do it yet."

Jordan rolled his eyes. "Get the helmet. I promise I'll make sure it's free of demon lice."

Raising my hand again, I shouted out in my mind for the helmet to come, but grew distracted partway. "Demons have lice?" I asked, and my helmet arrived.

It didn't fly into my hand but sort of rolled down the road in a defeated fashion. I leaned over and picked it up. There were a few minor dents, like it had fallen and risen and fallen against the pavement a few times, but the basic integrity of it was preserved. My mom probably would have had a few words to say on the matter, including irresponsible and poor life choices. Luckily, she wasn't here, so the helmet passed the test and was placed on my head after Jordan bleached it with his soul.

"We're working on soul magnification before I leave," he noted, and a red flag went off in my head as we took off down the road. When the day and the job were done, Jordan would be gone.

Sixteen

I couldn't be certain where we were going until we turned into the parking lot in front of a nursing home. My heart sank in my chest as Jordan slid into a parking spot and shed his helmet. Knowing I was expected to follow suit, I did, but I couldn't help but want to get as far away as possible. If this was where Giuseppe was, I didn't want to be around for what Jordan decided to do. Within every villain, there was a speck of humanity, and this was Giuseppe's.

The building was four stories and stretched out in an attempt to look like anything but the sterile prison it was. The doors slid open, and there was a pair of investigators from the medical examiner's office in the lobby speaking to a man and woman. Across from the small cut-off area was the front desk. An older woman with faux red hair and no eyebrows sat there staring at her hands mumbling to herself how this was the first time anything like this had happened on her watch. I didn't have to get anything else to know someone was dead, and somehow, I still hoped it wasn't Giuseppe's wife.

Jordan and I walked straight through a dining area filled with pills and the smell of chlorine, down a hallway and to the right. There were chairs everywhere and medical alerts on every wall. Electric doors with keypads blocked the ends of every hallway, but they opened right up for Jordan. He marched, with me on his heels, until we reached a small elevator in a corner. There were no stairs in sight. He pushed the single up button, and we waited.

"You're not going to hurt her, right?" I wanted to feel stupid even asking, but it had become a valid question.

"No—but I'm going to stop him from keeping her alive. He's been using minor demons to prolong her life." Jordan didn't look at me. It had to mean something. He didn't look at me, and the lady who was everything to a monster was going to die.

I shuffled a bit on the carpet. "He did this all for her, didn't he? Sacrificing Blake and Rio and Madrid and Deacon—this was all for her. If he had succeeded, would it have worked?"

"No."

"What do you mean no? He summoned a demon to get her back. He sold his soul," I whispered, then it hit me. "No... it wouldn't have worked."

"He did it for himself, and Mammon wouldn't have healed her no matter how much fine print Giuseppe added. Abelia—his wife—was dying a long time ago," Jordan whispered. The heat he had against the others was gone, and in their wake, there was only exhaustion and acceptance.

"He brought Madrid and Rio back," I pointed out as the elevator opened and we got on.

Jordan turned to face the door. "He had their souls, and he had ensured they both died. Demons can undo some of it, and he could have voided her illness, but Mammon would have done something. Blocked one of her arteries on the way out, put a hole in her heart—it would have ended either way, and she would have suffered—or worse, he would have become a demon."

"What? You said demons were angels."

When the doors opened, we walked out and turned to the left, going down the halls. Jordan was like a bloodhound on the trail, and I could only assume he had the right scent.

"Fallen angels," he corrected. "And most corrupted souls don't become demons—they become voids, but if a corrupted soul enters Hell while alive and in a body." Jordan shook his head. "I've only seen it happen once. It takes a long time, but it could happen."

"Hell's kind of like the house in Las Vegas," I noted.

Jordan didn't laugh. His face went stone cold as he turned a
door with a laminated name sign: *Abelia Farro*. The door slid
open, and the first part I saw was a chair drawn tight to the bed
in which Giuseppe sat holding tightly to a skeletal hand, weep-
ing. He wasn't the angry old man I had known. The cockiness
bordering on cruelty had fled, leaving a broken old man clinging
to his wife's hand sobbing as he pressed kisses against her paper
thin skin.

"Don't leave me," he pleaded to the woman. "*Mio amore—mio
angelo*, don't leave me here. Please." His voice cracked as he
caressed her face. "Don't leave me here without you."

"Giuseppe." Jordan's voice was soft, but even the slight noise
startled Giuseppe. He turned with bloodshot eyes glaring at us.

"Have you come to mock my failure?" he snarled like a cornered animal. "She's gone where I can never follow. Have you no
humanity? She could have lived. Kill me if you want, boy. There's
nothing left in this world worth living for."

Jordan shook his head. "If you'd let her go, you would have
had a chance to follow."

"Curse God and the Covenant! Send them both to Hell!
Why must we slave away to right a mistake the witch made? We
spend our lives hunting demons, and what do we get? Maybe
we'll end up in Heaven where the rest go naturally!" Giuseppe
scoffed. "Ha! What a joke!"

I fidgeted, wishing what Giuseppe said hadn't made so
much sense. Magic for your soul—it wasn't a fair trade. Then
again, I doubted the Devil made fair trades. Jordan moved slowly
forward, and the air crackled with tension.

"I think I can fix that for you," Jordan replied. He reached
forward, and Giuseppe reared back in his chair, dropping his
wife's hand.

"No! You need my permission, and I—" he stuttered as Jordan's hands touched his face.

The lights flickered, and the machines went haywire, but
there was no sound. A spark flew between Jordan's hands and
Giuseppe's face. A moment later, Jordan pulled away. Giuseppe
stared blankly ahead, not moving when Jordan turned and left. I

stalled for second, wondering what had just transpired, before following.

"What did you do?" I asked.

"I took his magic," Jordan replied returning to the elevator and pressing the down button.

My eyes flickered back toward the room then Jordan. "That's it? He leads four people to their deaths—personally attempts to kill at least two, but—no problem—they were rogues, so bye-bye magic, and he's off the hook?"

Jordan spun to face me. "His wife is dead. Now he has no magic. Death would have been kinder. Unlike you, most of us don't have a chance to live in the modern world. Without magic, he can't pay his bills or get food. It'd be like cutting off a mortal's hands. So, yes, Jon, that's it."

I stood stunned and mutely trailed after Jordan when the elevator doors opened. A life without magic was no life at all for Giuseppe. If Hell was a state of being, he had entered a prison running on the same rules.

"Why him?" I asked.

Jordan stormed off toward the front door. "Why him what?"

"Madrid dies, Rio dies, and Blake dies. Why does Giuseppe live?"

Jordan sighed, shoving his hands in his pockets as we strolled out into the air and headed toward the bike. "Are you even paying attention? Mammon killed them. He took their souls out. When they started moving again—it wasn't their souls going back in. They were more like meat puppets than souls. It was just semantics."

"Okay, and Blake? Did Mammon do something to his wound?" I asked. Jordan shook his head, staring up at the night sky. "Then why did he die?"

"He was going to kill himself."

I blanched. "What?"

Jordan sat down on the edge of his motorcycle and clasped his hands. "He was going to kill himself, Jon. He had just had it confirmed his wife was gone for good. He was going to commit suicide."

"But—couldn't he redeem his soul? Couldn't he hunt the demons with claims to his soul and do some charity work or something?" There had to be some kind of redemption. If the Covenant was fair, I couldn't know if God was fairer than the Devil, but if he was, we deserved as many second chances as the rest of humanity. Jordan nodded, and I pushed on. "Then why would he kill himself?"

"He killed a man. Deacon Sullivan was on his soul, and the cost was a stain he didn't have the strength to wash out," Jordan replied.

"What about Deacon? All he did was summon a demon. You said it was for his son." I shoved my hands in my pockets, hoping there was some sort of moral to this story. Somehow, I had wanted the good guys to be purely good and not just the better of two evils like the rest of the world.

Jordan stood and handed me the helmet I had been using. "He couldn't have gotten his son, but he will save who knows how many children because Mammon can't step foot on Earth for a decade. It's worth something."

I got onto the back of the motorcycle as Jordan put on his helmet, and we were off. The tension had mounted, crested, and fallen. There was nothing but downhill from here until who knows when, and for the time being, I was okay with it. I didn't have the heart to hunt rogues. Demons—those guys were bad and evil in a clear cut way in which nobody lost. Demons didn't have families, and they had earned their place in Hell. If Belial was anything to go by, death was a welcomed relief. We arrived back in front of my dorm, and I swung my leg over the bike, stepping toward my building before pulling the helmet off and holding it out to Jordan, who shook his head.

"You dented it. It's your problem now," he said.

I smiled in spite of myself. "Thanks."

"Don't thank me. It's useless without a bike," Jordan pointed out. "Keep practicing your shields."

"Wow, just—'keep practicing your shields,' and you get to ride off into the sunset? You're off, and I go back to being a fake normal?" I couldn't help but feel underwhelmed.

Jordan didn't answer. He just revved the engine and flew off into the night. Holding the helmet against my side, I scanned into the building. The stairs were empty, and the intense sound of late night studying encompassed the entire building in an eerie silence. It was entirely unnatural. Trudging back to my room, I kicked off my shoes. Tyson had his headphones on as he stared down at his geology textbook. Though I probably should have studied, I threw my shirt and jeans into my laundry bin, and burrowed beneath the covers in my boxers. The building was a sauna, so pajama pants were out. Curling up, I flipped over to face the wall. The hunt was completed. So why didn't I feel relieved?

Seventeen

Warren G. Harding coined a term following World War I to sum up the desire of the American people: a return to normalcy. However, the phrase wasn't exactly what he'd said. Harding originally stated, "Americas present need is not heroics, but healing; not nostrums, but normalcy." This was what I needed, or so I thought. The first day had me watching newspapers and news stations online wondering when the bodies would surface. They weren't exactly hidden, yet nothing came in the first day or the second. A week passed without me seeing Jordan, and school had never felt so dull. Classes were winding down toward exams, and I was staring at business class after economic class after mathematics wondering when everything I wanted to do with my life became mundane. My return to normalcy was not what I wanted, so I knew I had to do something.

I found my way back to the shop at the beginning of exam week after my last Monday exam. The exterior was the same bright hue—fuchsia apparently, according to the internet. The sign swung with an annoying creak as I walked up those same three, slightly crooked steps to the same tiny knob sparkling beneath the afternoon sunlight. Opening the door, I stepped inside. The angel rang, and there the similarities stopped. A man reading on the floor glanced up while a man and woman continued chatting at the table in the bay window. A few shoppers wove between the bookshelves. With Jordan, the shop had been a step outside of the norm. Now, it was just another bookstore.

"Can I help you?" an older man called from the counter.

He had bright blue eyes and obscenely white hair parted to one side. His cheek bones were prominent and the gauntness beneath them was the only difference between him and the picture on the wall behind. He smiled, and I wasn't sure what I could say.

"You're looking for Jordan, aren't you?" The grin on his face grew. "Jonathan, I presume."

I walked toward the counter. "Yeah, Jon, and you are..."

"Solomon Morgan—at your service," he replied stretching out a hand to clasp my own. We shook hands, and I couldn't stop myself.

"What did you keep in the back room to scare Mam—"

Solomon Morgan shushed me. "He may be gone, but we do not speak the name lightly. I suppose a student without a proper teacher couldn't possibly know not to." He flashed his white teeth in a quick smile. "I'm a purveyor of Greek fire. Though I've always enjoyed chemistry, certain ones should be mixed..." He paused abruptly; his eyes narrowed. "You're looking for Jordan, but let us question why."

"I—" I faltered and gave up. "I wanted to say goodbye before he left."

"Well then." His eyes sparkled. "He's already left."

There it was. My life would be me not completely trained, knowing there was this whole world of demon hunting I would never fully be a part of despite my magic. Part of me was relieved, but the rest of me was certain I got a raw deal. I could do basic wards, and I had a rather subpar basic training. Most of what I could do was more my continued dedication to practice than anything else. In theory, the amulet would work as I would never know how to summon a demon, but I wanted to go further. Maybe magic just worked quietly. It was a temptation lurking beneath the surface. Inside, magic slammed down, tearing apart everything until there was only wanting and emptiness until the next hit. Maybe Tyson was right. Maybe I had been dragged into a drug.

"Do you teach?" I asked slowly, and Morgan shook his head.

"I know." He tapped the side of his head. "But I don't have the talent."

The slight hope sank. "Oh, guess that's it then. Thanks."

I turned to leave when Morgan cleared his throat. "Jonathan?" I looked back at him. There was a small note card in between his forefinger and middle finger. "He left this for you." I was back to the counter reaching for the note before I could even fully process there was a note to be had. Morgan laughed and set the card down on the counter. "Choose carefully," he said.

The card was simple and the writing a quick jot across the paper said: "Message me if interested in a summer hunt. Finish your exams and talk to your mother. It will be international—update your passport."

"Thanks," I said and swaggered out toward the dorm with the note in my hand. A summer hunt—I sent a text to him inquiring about details, and my phone rang.

"All demons," Jordan said when I picked up.

I sighed in relief. "I'll talk to my mom and get everything ready."

"Concentrate on your exams first. It's not like I won't be back to help contain the mess the summoning made," he said then hung up.

My heart soared. Every bit of me was ecstatic, and I knew I had to go. The university was not the apex for me anymore. From the moment I found another person with magic, I had found my new normal. The possibility of the world having at least three hundred and some more was an impossible dream realized. There was also the brilliant—and yet to be destroyed by Jordan—chance my father was out there somewhere still alive. If he lived, I would find him. I was just a few tests away from getting back to my normalcy: a demon hunter's apprentice.

About the Author

Eli Celata was born in Rochester and is currently attending Binghamton University as a doctoral student.

Clean Reads

ALL STORY, NO GUILT.